AfterW

"A Sense of Foreboding on a Summer's Evening"

AfterWitch

"A Sense of Foreboding on a Summer's Evening"

Cover Artwork by Hannah Taggart
https://www.saatchiart.com/taggart
Cover Concept: James Stoorie
ISBN: 978-1-6780-8816-3

"Guide me through the end of my teenage years with safety"

June Gibbons

AfterWitch

Chapter One: Strawberries for Tea

Sour, the same as the summer so far.

Tea grimaced at the taste of the spoiled fruit, glancing around to see if anyone was looking before turning aside to spit the strawberry out into the dirt. She felt a sliver slip down her chin, smeared like a trail of blood.

"Oh, classy" sneered Amber Stone. "It's all about class with you, isn't it Tea?"

Of course, she should have realised that nothing she did would escape Amber's attention. Why was she always watching her? It's not as though they were friends, far from it, particularly after all that business with Jack. If anything, Tea sensed a scarcely restrained hostility emanating from Amber, who appeared to be constantly biting her lip in Tea's presence, as if to say what she really felt would somehow break the spell. This only made it the more annoying that Amber insisted on addressing her by her nickname, a privilege supposedly reserved for family and close friends. 'Miss Felicity Greene to you' Tea had wanted to haughtily retort. Yet, as usual, she said nothing, resigned to shrugging her shoulders and attempting to act nonchalant, anything to give the impression that Amber's opinions held no power over her.

"Anyway, as I was saying, I invited him over…" Amber, feigning sudden disinterest, switched her attention back to the girl in the sunhat who stood next to her.

Disengaged from Tea, the two launched into an intense, whispered conversation, swinging their empty baskets as they sauntered off along the furrow, stooping occasionally to pick a strawberry or two. Shielding her eyes, she watched them go, the girls silhouetted against a glinting sun sinking with fatigue as the afternoon wore on. Returning to her work, Tea struggled down the row in the opposite direction, dragging a basket heavy with strawberries that rolled and tumbled about, the majority already split and bruised. Why did Amber take such an interest in her life, or at least pretend to? It was not as though Tea had anything to offer. Unlike her, Amber had been one of the most popular girls at school, as well as being from one of the most privileged backgrounds. Which, come to think of it, only added to the mystery. Why would Amber take a summer job at Withers Fruit Farm? She hardly needed the money, certainly not the pittance to be earned here. Surely, with her family ties, if she had the sudden desire to pick fruit, Amber could land a much cushier deal? A vineyard in the south of France or something? At least she had a choice, whereas for Tea this was a necessity, especially since her mum got sick. This was hardly how she had envisaged spending her first summer out of school, but the most important thing was to stick to 'The Plan'. If Tea were to follow in her sister's footsteps and start a new life outside the village then she needed to start saving. Unfortunately, job opportunities were so few and far between around Blight that she had to accept anything going, just like those hop pickers from Victorian times she had read about.

The trudge back to The Farm Shop always felt as though it took forever, even longer on sultry days like this with the flat, endless aisles of the plantation seeming to sprawl to an impossibly distant horizon. Stumbling over dry clods of earth and limp, straggling greenery, Tea fell into further brooding over Amber. What was behind this strange fascination she now held for her one-time nemesis? Previously, Amber had barely deigned to acknowledge her, that is apart from making the occasional snide, dismissive remark about 'The Greene Children' not really being 'our kind', as though Tea and her sister had crawled out of a hole in the ground. Once Amber had even confronted Tea in the school corridor and accused her of thinking 'you are better than us', which was certainly not the case. In fact, most of the time, she felt the complete opposite. So why, since the start of the summer, had their lives become inseparable?

Tea was beginning to feel flustered in the oppressive heat, her shoulder aching at the weight of the basket, the familiar restlessness rising within. Was Amber a spy? Perhaps she had been planted by someone in authority to keep Tea under surveillance, to monitor her every move? No, no, that was just her imagination, her mind playing tricks again. Tea took a deep breath, mentally reciting the incantation she had assimilated from her reading: 'I will not allow my emotions to escalate, I will not invent drama to feel more important, I will not view the world as a threatening place'. If truth be told, no doubt Amber's motives were much more mundane...

Perhaps she had genuinely been after Jack all along? Tea had assumed Amber had merely been stirring things up, yet even when they were meant to be together Jack had been unable to stop himself making all those sly little comments to Tea, implying that there was something between him and Amber. Tea could never be sure whether this was the truth. Jack would pass off these remarks as jokes designed to make her jealous, but there had been a heartlessness in his tone that hurt. Still, the idea that someone like Amber could be envious of her seemed absurd. Besides, she must know by now that Tea and Jack were history. Nobody could keep a secret for long in 'Dear Old Blighty'. People's boredom around here was such that they seized upon any gossip about your private life like ravenous dogs, spreading it around the village like a plague. Maybe Amber had won? Maybe she and Jack were now an item? In which case Amber had even less reason to feel wary of Tea, so that made absolutely no sense at all. With her free hand, Tea scratched anxiously at her chin, hoping she had removed any trace of the red stain from earlier.

The Farm Shop was nothing more elaborate than a ramshackle barn encircled by a few outhouses, that stood, lopsided, in the middle of an open field. A few years back the Withers family had partitioned it in two and the smaller section out front, the area open to customers, had at least seen a little renovation, in the shape of a lick of paint and a patching of the more gaping holes in the roof. Staff like Tea were expected to remain out of sight, sticking to the rundown part of the premises round the back, where the storerooms and packing areas were housed. But today, following her extended trek across the fields, Tea was relieved to step out of the blazing sun into the dingy, solemn shade of the barn, a sensation like passing into the body of a church. She deposited her latest basket onto one of the trestle tables for sorting and inspection which, to her dismay, was this afternoon being supervised by Mick Withers, youngest son of the farmer.

Withers Junior had been two years above Tea at school but was older than that implied; it was common knowledge he had been kept back a few times. Rumour had it his father was on the brink of disinheriting Mick, forced to abandon any ideas that his last born would successfully expand the family's farming industry following a series of disastrous ventures that proved Mick lacked even the most basic business acumen. So this is where he had ended up, in spite of all of his advantages - assistant manager at The Farm Shop. Mick Withers reminded Tea of one of those stupid sons in fairy-tales who always fail at their quests, which made it very difficult to keep a straight face whenever he attempted to assert his authority.

"What's that mark on your face?" he immediately demanded on reaching Tea's table, puffing up his scrawny frame as best he could. "How many times do I have to tell you…staff are not permitted to sample the fruit!"

"It's a rash!" countered Tea with a wounded expression. "Actually, I'm very sensitive about it. I must be allergic to the stupid plants!"

"Then maybe it's time you started looking for a job elsewhere…" Mick Withers muttered under his breath, although without conviction, as if instantly undermined by the mild challenge Tea had presented. Nevertheless, on glancing down at her consignment, he did not shed his look of distaste.

"Look at the state of this batch Greene! I doubt half of them are edible. Do you deliberately pick the rotten fruit just to annoy me? Nobody else here seems to have your problems…"

To be fair to Mick Withers, overlooking that whole failed 'alpha male' façade, he never threatened to fire her. And he would be perfectly within his rights to do so. Tea was all too aware that the bulk of her harvest did not meet acceptable standards, although she could not grasp the reason why. Every strawberry simply seemed to spoil at her touch, to perish the moment she plucked it, decaying in the time it took her to deliver it from the fields. "You must be cursed" her friend Karmilla had joked, although Tea's smile had soon faded. In her defence, Tea could point out that the work rate of Amber and her cronies was far worse, yet Mick Withers went out of his way to make excuses for them. But then everybody knew this was only because Mick had a crush on Amber, trailing around behind her like a lost puppy, taking every opportunity to pay a clumsy compliment. Recently he had even tried to ingratiate himself with her mother, canvassing for Mrs Stone during her successful bid to be elected a local councillor. Needless to say, the other staff were not treated to the leniency bestowed upon Amber. Wages were calculated by the weighted amount of serviceable produce supplied and, by the time Mick Withers had sifted out all her useless pickings, Tea knew she would, once again, be sent home with reduced pay. "Strawberry short changed" as Karmilla had put it yesterday. At this rate, Tea would never be able to afford to move away.

After collecting the scant earnings she was entitled to, Tea crossed to an adjacent shack that served as a washroom for female employees. Dousing her face with cold water, she finally succeeded in eradicating the faint red mark that had clung so stubbornly to her chin since she had taken a bite out of that strawberry. Church bells carrying from afar confirmed it was now six o'clock and time to head home. Tea, keen to avoid Amber and company, collected her bag, phone and current book from her locker before setting out on a circuitous route around the parched, wilted fields. On reaching the perimeter of the farm, she spotted Karmilla up ahead, leaning against a telegraph pole at the side of the lane and serenely smoking a rolled cigarette, watching their fellow workers filtering past. She must have been waiting, as she waved to Tea as soon as she came idling out of the gate.

"Until now, I was working in the left field, but I thought I saw you" smiled Karmilla, in her near perfect, accented English. "How is your mother?"

13

As strange as it may sound, considering they had only known each other a few weeks, Tea already counted Karmilla as her closest friend. Although Karmilla was a couple of years older and came from a completely different background, Tea had established an instant connection with her, something she had singularly failed to do with the local teenagers. Sure there were kids from school that she could hang out with, drinking in the park or sitting on the stairs at stupid house parties, but she felt she had little in common with any of them. When she was alone, Tea blamed herself. There had been close friendships with girls and boys in the past, but perhaps they had been too intimate, too intense? Those kinds of relationships seemed to pose a problem for Tea and always burnt themselves out early on, leaving her dependent on a circle of passing acquaintances. So when Karmilla had arrived at Withers Farm and struck up a conversation, Tea had treated the meeting as a fresh start, an opportunity to do things right. Naturally her new friend was not planning to stay in the village for long, she was just earning some 'easy money' over the summer so that she could put down a deposit on a place in the city, where her long-term boyfriend, also from Romania, would be joining her. But at least this way Tea herself could leave Blight with some good memories of her final few months here and, who knows, it may be that she and Karmilla kept in touch. Together, they strolled off down the lane. Beneath her brusque manner, Karmilla's kindness was apparent in the way she always asked after Tea's mum, which none of their neighbours ever remembered to do.

"No change, really. She's still at the clinic and I feel I'm getting nowhere. The staff won't tell me anything. It's like they resent me asking questions…"

About a month ago, towards the end of the school term, Tea's mum had suddenly been taken sick. There had been no warning signs and the day before she seemed perfectly healthy, or as healthy as could be expected for a social worker required to work ridiculous hours whilst existing on a diet of crisps and cigarettes. Then had come that terrible morning when she couldn't get out of bed. At dawn she had called for

14

Tea, trying but failing to control the rising panic in her voice. She had probably suffered in silence for hours, awaking in the middle of the night to discover she had been stricken with paralysis. Trying not to hyperventilate, Tea had made a barely comprehensible call to the local GP and within half an hour Dr Chalk, a pallid waxwork of a man, had materialised on their doorstep. "Felicity…" he had greeted her formally.

Dr Chalk spent twenty minutes prodding at her mum and interrogating her about her symptoms whilst Tea loitered awkwardly at the bedroom door. It was late last night her mum had first noticed something was wrong, her body going numb and tingling all over, as though she were being pricked with pins. Despite appearing to respond without emotion, which Tea put down to his professional detachment, Dr Chalk was evidently concerned enough to make an urgent referral to his private practice. There had once been a small NHS hospital on the boundaries of Blight, covering the immediate area, but that had long since been shut down due to lack of funds. Now the only option was a private clinic situated some miles away, in which Dr Chalk was a partner, although he resided locally. And so, early upon that early summer's morning, Tea's mum had been whisked away in an ambulance. There was nothing to worry about, both Tea's mum and the doctor had insisted, no need for Tea to accompany them to the clinic. Sitting her exam that day, that was the most important thing. Tea had not seen or spoken to her mother since.

"Every time I've called the clinic, they tell me my mum can't come to the phone, that she is slipping in out of consciousness and is no condition to receive visitors…" Tea confided to Karmilla. "And I only ever seem to speak to this same nurse, Hall I think her name is. She is so rude to me, so abrupt, you would not believe it. She always makes me feel like I am wasting her valuable time, when all I want is a few answers, like anyone would in my situation. How cruel is that? And this person is supposed to be a nurse…"

As they walked, deliberately keeping their distance from others wandering the same route home, Karmilla sympathised with Tea over her recent misfortunes. Following the breakup with Jack and all this trauma with her mum, the last thing she needed was to face such hostility from staff at the clinic. Perhaps they could write a strongly worded complaint, Karmilla proposed, and they fell about laughing as they fantasised about all the insults they would include. What Tea was not yet able to share with her friend was the guilt she had been feeling over her mum's illness, or rather her personal reaction to it. Ashamed as she was to admit such thoughts, a part of Tea was mad at her mother, holding her responsible for deserting her youngest daughter at such a difficult time. If only everything didn't revolve around money, but with her mum unable to work and private nursing bills to be paid for, Tea could see what little savings she had would soon drain away. And then who would look after the house? Or Whispers or Noosha or Hopscotch? Unless things had changed by autumn, 'The Plan' would have to be put on hold indefinitely.

"Why don't you ask Elsie to help? Isn't that what big sisters are for?" suggested Karmilla, who secretly longed for a sister herself.

"Ha! Yes, you're right. I will speak to Sea tonight…"

Seeking seclusion, the girls took a detour down a solitary lane, the kind that only seems to come to life during the summer. Hidden from sight behind towering hedgerows, with only the occasional drift of their voices or the echo of their footfalls to give them away, anyone working in an adjoining field might be startled by such sounds, convinced for an instant that the tales were true and this stretch of road really was haunted. Although early evening was approaching, still the heat haze simmered, and Tea rubbed her eyes as if to dispel a mirage. But it was not just the bees, or the insects that darted to and from the nettled verges; this entire, enclosed environment appeared to waver and hum to a low current, an undertow, as though they were passing beneath electricity pylons. Tea steered the conversation away from her mother, asking for tips on her mock driving test tomorrow and casually mentioning the last time she had seen Jack, at that sleepout in the woods. Karmilla had never met Tea's ex yet was unimpressed by the character sketches she had been given. Dismissing his name with a look of indifference, Karmilla discussed her own dreams about relocating to the city, urging Tea to accompany her as soon as she could. Cristian would join them on returning from his travels around Europe and, finally, Karmilla would have a place to call home; she had been estranged from her 'too religious, too strict' parents for years.

They reached a turning where the path split in two, beckoning travellers in opposing directions like a maze. For a minute Karmilla looked lost, disorientated by the twists and turns they had taken.

"This place is still so strange, so confusing to me…" she half joked.

Exchanging a brief hug, Tea promised to text Karmilla tomorrow with the outcome of her test. These moments were charged with a perhaps inappropriate amount of emotion for Tea. At times she felt she wanted to cling tightly to her friend; to freeze the summer at its height and keep Karmilla in Blight forever. But she knew she must fight to control these violent forces at work within her, to stop them ever becoming known to anyone but herself. Karmilla lit a second cigarette and veered off to the right. She was renting a bedsit close to the centre of the village, located off what was optimistically known as the 'High Street'. Perhaps this had once been a bustling thoroughfare, a hive of industry, but all that remained these days were a cluster of convenience stores and charity shops, interspersed with the odd greasy café or old-fashioned hairdressers. Not forgetting the local library of course, where Tea had a second job whenever it could afford to open. Karmilla turned to blow a kiss from a distance, then forged on ahead.

Tea watched her friend go, lingering alone in the lane until she was sure Karmilla was out of sight. From here it was a further twenty-minute walk home, which involved leaving the path to follow the twisting trails leading up through the trees of HarmWood. Yet, this evening, the journey could wait. There was something that needed attending to first. Unseen, Tea ducked through the camouflaged opening in the hedge that acted as a shortcut to the churchyard. She had made her mind up earlier; today she was going to pay her dad a surprise visit.

Chapter Two: The Veil House

They used to come here a lot when Tea was young, but never on a Sunday. Her mum seemed to prefer the charms of the churchyard when there was nobody else about, usually a late afternoon or mid Saturday morning. Not that there was really anything to see; there was nothing special about her dad's grave. In her imagination, Tea would romanticize the setting, envisioning herself drawing back the ivy from some weather-beaten cross concealed in an overgrown corner, vainly attempting to decipher the cryptic inscription. Yet, in reality, Gary Greene's resting place looked modern and unremarkable, a small plaque set in a neat row alongside other members of his extended family. The epitaph simply stated his name and dates, not even stretching to a 'beloved father of', which was common on other markers. Tea supposed what she really wanted was for her father's grave to give her some idea of his personality, their shared identity, seeing as she had barely been old enough to remember him. Unfortunately, such a revelation had so far not been forthcoming, even though she had waited so patiently. Since the age of two, in fact.

If it seemed unlike her mother to neglect to add some poetic flourish or intricate design to the stone, Tea had later discovered this was because the Greene family had not allowed her any say in the funeral arrangements; a feud that continued to this day. Tea had never divined the precise nature of the dispute but, although her paternal grandparents lived locally, only on the outskirts of Blight, she had never had a relationship with them. This seldom troubled her as a child, considering she had never known her mum's family either. Yet, as she grew older, at times Tea began to resent being left in the dark. From what she could gather from Sea, their mother had been brought up abroad but beyond that the details were sketchy, the conversation inevitably closed down.

So, what did she expect to find here? The key to some mystery about herself? Even pretending to treat that idea as a joke made her squirm with embarrassment, which might explain why she had kept these visits a secret, not only from her family but also Jack and Karmilla. Nonetheless, despite the sense of shame that sometimes gripped her, that ache of being an impostor at the graveside, in recent years Tea had been drawn back to the churchyard with increasing regularity. But she always came here alone, to be alone among the stones, just like Lucy in 'Dracula'.

What were originally family outings to the grave had ceased for several reasons. For a start, by the time she was a teenager Tea had become bored accompanying her mum by herself. At three years her senior, Sea had already stopped going. To be honest, even when they were younger, tending the grave did not hold their interest for long. After a while they would be allowed to wander off and play, exploring the monuments or chasing each other around the church in different directions. With hindsight, Tea realised she had welcomed this distraction from the detachment she felt, her guilt at being unable to share her mother's grief for a father she had never known. Yet perhaps for Sea, being older, the motives had been more complex. Tea recalled times during their games that her sister had suddenly burst into tears for no reason, distressed beyond the thrill of the chase, the stitch in her side. Maybe all the running and shouting had been an attempt by Sea to escape, to express her genuine hurt?

Another reason the sisters had stopped coming was because of what happened to their mementos. Under their mum's supervision, every week they would sit at the kitchen table fashioning little ornaments, pretty trinkets and tiny figurines, with which to decorate the grave. Sometimes they would bottle up these objects and bury them in the surrounding earth, sometimes they would simply hide them in the grass. However, too often when they returned the following week they would find their gifts had been removed or, even worse, damaged beyond repair. On one infamous and humiliating occasion their mum had got into an argument with the groundskeeper when they had caught him burning their 'offerings' on the bonfire. Following that incident, the sisters had gradually grown disenchanted with these excursions, finding excuses to be elsewhere. Thankfully, their mum seemed prepared to let the matter rest. And that was that. Until, one morning, many years later, when Tea had woken up in a peculiar mood. Without explanation, she felt an overwhelming need to visit the churchyard that very day. And this compulsion had seized her at random intervals ever since, just like it had this morning.

The piece of land where the Greene family plots lay was far too exposed for Tea's liking, leaving her open to the prying eyes of parishioners and passing acquaintances. What if she needed to run for cover? So, rather than kneeling at her dad's grave, she always selected the same rickety bench set back against the dry-stone wall, where she could sit unnoticed in the shade of a cedar tree, encircled by a barricade of gorse bushes, like one of those sleeping princesses in storybooks. From this vantage point she still had a clear view of the grave, should her father's poor, tormented spirt ever decide to rise from the dead. Actually, there had been nights in the past when, stumbling home after a few drinks, Tea had half expected to encounter his ghost stalking the country lanes he been so familiar with throughout his life. Yet here in the churchyard, the atmosphere exuded peace and contentment, something she rarely experienced within herself.

Tea appreciated that her vigils may appear weird for her age, however she had really grown to treasure the solitude of this setting. It gave her the opportunity to reflect on the day's events and compose herself for whatever lay ahead. Foremost in her mind was her mock driving test tomorrow morning, which she remained convinced she was going to fail. But also, always there in the background, was the constant, nagging unease over what was happening to her mum. When she got home, Tea would seek her sister's advice regarding the clinic and Nurse Hall's obstructive behaviour. Sea would know what to do. She had a gift for seeing things clearly and a natural charisma that could win over the sternest opponents. Yes, contrary to what Amber Stone might try and insinuate, Sea had always been sociable and popular, much more so than Tea. Men and women appeared almost impulsively attracted to her, instinctively recognising her inner strength and beauty, something they must sense as inherently lacking in her little sister.

Perhaps Sea had tried to contact her earlier for an update? The reception around Blight was so bad she may have been unable to get through on Tea's phone. It was just another example of how backward this place was, like they longed to return to the Dark Ages. Softly humming an old song they had sung here as children, Tea contemplated the dusk settling over the churchyard, the rolling hills beyond. With a sigh of resignation, she rose to her feet. Tranquillity like this never lasted; she must get back before the light failed.

Retracing her route along the edge of a cornfield, Tea emerged from the undergrowth and stepped back out at the spot where she had parted from Karmilla only an hour or so earlier. For a short distance she followed the lane, gradually drifting across from one side to the other as it wound its way through the wilds. Here, where the trees made their stately descent to meet the tarmac, Tea abruptly turned aside, entering the woods. The steep, immediate incline always took her by surprise no matter how times she hiked this trail, forcing her to catch her breath. Yet Tea would reach home in half the time by cutting cross country, climbing the ill-defined track to overlook the scattered, detached properties of her nearest neighbours. Occasionally this had obliged her to return a friendly wave when they had caught her peering down into their back gardens. There were various landmarks along the route, which levelled out after the initial ascent - a brake full of gutted cars; the vast, blackened scar of an old bonfire, long since extinguished and perhaps a relic of a party she had never been invited to. And, at approximately mid-point, deep in the heart of HarmWood, stood The Veil House.

The Veil House was never welcoming, yet at dusk it appeared only more withdrawn, the way that people will sometimes withdraw into their darkest thoughts. Set further back in the trees than the other piles Tea had passed and elevated on a grassy ridge slightly above the track, the dilapidated structure was closely confined on all sides by unbroken woodland. How old was she now? Still, even after all these years, Tea felt her stomach drop whenever she passed beneath those inky, staring windows. However, she would not permit herself to break into a run, just like as a child she had refused to flinch when the other kids had dared her to enter. Tea seemed to remember her turn had come around far too often; perhaps she was being picked on or perhaps her so-called friends, congregated behind her in a semi-circle, were actually more scared than she was. In contrast, she had always felt a thrill rather than fear when approaching the door; the door that seemed to be kept permanently ajar. A *frisson,* was that the right word for the feeling? There were times she had barely been able to suppress a grin as she crossed the threshold. Well, some things never change, Tea had to admit it. Now as then, she felt drawn to The Veil House, as though someone or something inside was calling to her, longing to communicate some connection they shared, a secret she alone had forgotten. But, wait. Those childhood adventures had all taken place during the day and, in the dusk, The Veil House was a different prospect. Its appearance was no longer just inhospitable, but hostile. Any sunlight that once filtered forlornly through the surrounding trees had now faded, turning the dense frame of foliage a dark, sombre green. No wonder the children of Blight had chosen this as their local 'haunted house'. There were plenty of other derelict properties dotted around the village, abandoned by the wealthy or wise when they relocated, but none looked quite as forbidding at this hour as The Veil House.

It was getting cold. Tea shivered and hurried on down the trail, dismissing any feelings of déjà vu summoned up by The Veil House; fleeting memories of cobwebbed corridors, cold fireplaces and a ruined conservatory with a tree growing up through the roof. Fortunately, there was not much further to go before she reached 'The Burrows'. Their family home had allegedly been named after an ancient legend which claimed a warren of catacombs lay secreted underneath the house. If this story sounded unlikely, then it hadn't stopped Tea and her sister spending a few summer holidays fruitlessly seeking a way in. Yet 'The Burrows' did have a history, which had made the tales seem more plausible back then. In olden days, Tea had been told the lodge belonged to a gatekeeper or warden of an estate, although the manor house it served must have been demolished long ago.

The woodland trail emerged from the trees and ran straight into The Greene's back garden, an untended jungle that her mum was always meaning to 'get someone to have a look at'. This meant weaving your way through wild rhododendrons and clambering over toppled rose trellises in order to reach the doorstep. As she searched for her keys, Tea cast a parting glance back over the garden which, in her wake, seemed to gently exhale as it fell under the gathering spell of night. There was no sign of Hopscotch anywhere, but maybe that was a good thing; she only ever seemed to appear when something dramatic was about to happen. The last time Tea had seen her had been the evening her mum fell ill.

Keys successfully retrieved from the bottom of her bag, Tea opened the back door to the familiar mewl from within and the sound of her cat, Whispers, leaping down from the kitchen surface.

"I'm sorry for leaving you alone so long…I had to be somewhere else…" Tea explained as she stroked the jet-black fur to an appreciative purr. "But we understand each other, don't we?"

She did not know why, yet she always felt the need to apologise whenever she was fixed by the glimmer of those fearless green eyes.

With Whispers fed and pampered, Tea embarked on what had become her typical evening routine since being left to her own devices. Although hardly a domestic goddess herself, her mum would be proud. With no Jack to distract her Tea had transformed herself into quite the perfect housewife, dusting and hoovering each room on a regular basis, washing and ironing in the middle of the night. Understandably, she found it necessary to spice up these mundane chores a bit. Music had to be blaring out in the background and, if she took the occasional slug from one of the sherry bottles standing neglected in the drinks cabinet, well, nobody lived close enough to know. By far Tea's favourite task was to ensure that Noosha's supplies were laid out on the front lawn. This involved a complex juggling act, manoeuvring saucers of leftover cat food and slices of apple, plus a plastic bowl brimming with water, all the way from the kitchen to a sheltered nook just off the drive. Once outside, Tea would deposit the items and wait. The Greene's front garden was not really a garden as such, more a wide patch of rough grass enclosed by trees that would loom and rustle restlessly after dark. A gravel track led for a half mile from their door, through the woods and out onto the road. Perhaps the lawn was too exposed for a fox to feel comfortable, as it was rare for Noosha to appear in Tea's presence. Sometimes though, the wait would be rewarded, the vixen slipping stealthily from the undergrowth into the starlight.

"My friend, you've come back…" On such precious evenings, Noosha would politely tolerate herself to be petted and was patient with Tea when she lapsed into baby talk. However, there was no time to wait for Noosha's appearance tonight. There were things to do and Tea needed to be up early tomorrow.

Didn't she used to go to parties? These days, by the time she had finished all her duties, all Tea wanted to do was curl up quietly with a book, vaguely aware of the clock ticking slowly towards midnight. She was currently reading 'Goblin Market'. Next, it would be 'Tess Of The D'Urbervilles' again. Jack had always complained her taste in books was 'weird' or 'depressing'. He never seemed to read at all, despite coming from the sort of family where the father has a study. Yet this evening Tea could not allow herself such a luxury; before she could sit down she must speak to her sister and resolve the issue with the clinic. She poured a generous glass of her mother's sherry and grabbed her phone, hoping that she would be able to get a signal.

"Hi, Sea, can you hear me?"

At first, white noise or possibly the north wind, like putting a conch to your ear.

"Hi, Tea! Yes, I can hear you, can you hear me? Sorry I haven't been in touch. I meant to call but you know how it is. Everything seems so crazy right now…"

Busy, always too busy. That was the problem with Sea nowadays, she was forever preoccupied, either due to work assignments or her exciting new social life. Whatever the reason, you sensed she wasn't really listening. Tea knew what people would say, that she was just jealous, but those were the kind of people who never found time themselves. All she wanted was for her sister to acknowledge that this was a challenging phase for the family, that they needed her support and her attention, if only in the short term. Was that too much to ask? Whilst she dare not express it out loud, for fear she had read the situation wrong, recently Tea had felt as though her sister's new opportunities had turned her a little selfish. That said, she recognised how much she relied upon Sea's common sense and, currently, bearing in mind her sister's job involved processing blood tests at a city hospital, also her insight into dealing with difficult medical staff.

When Tea relayed her conflicts with the clinic her sister reassured her, insisting she was completely within her rights to visit their mum regardless of whether she was conscious or not, although Sea raised suspicions about the patient's supposed condition. Thus, with a bit of gentle persuasion, Tea was quickly convinced that her best option was to simply turn up tomorrow unannounced and demand a diagnosis as well as an apology from this Nurse Hall, preferably in front of Dr Chalk. Any problems, they could always seek a second opinion. Sea herself promised she would make every effort to visit just as soon as she could arrange cover at work. She wished Tea good luck with her driving test ("Do you still have that creepy instructor? What was his name?"), before apologising that she really had to go. During their conversation Tea had wandered into the kitchen and, on ending the call, happened to glance out of the window. Poised there, barely discernible in the gloom of the back garden, crouched a small, dark shape.

'Hopscotch!" Tea gasped as she wrestled open the door, needing to prove to herself that the errant hare really had returned.

For a breathless few seconds they both stayed still and silent, observing each other in suspension, like statues. The hare blinked once or twice and twitched its nose but otherwise remained rooted to the spot. To call Hopscotch a pet would be too generous, yet perhaps she was demonstrating her loyalty by making such appearances, reminding Tea that she would be close at hand if ever she were needed. True, her visits were not always welcome. Sightings of Hopscotch could presage positive events, like the night Tea first got together with Jack or the evening prior to Karmilla's arrival, but they more frequently seemed to signal some disaster was pending. As expected, the instant Tea made a move to, cautiously, step down into the garden, Hopscotch turned tail and fled back into the foliage. Bemused, Tea retreated into the kitchen, firmly locking the door behind her. Suddenly, she was prickling with a presentiment that something significant was about to happen; a sense of foreboding on a summer's evening. All around her, 'The Burrows' groaned and sighed with life, as though there were other, unseen residents moving about. But then, the old house often made sounds like that, she noticed it more now she was alone.

Tea attempted to talk herself down. Why would anyone else be here? It was hardly as if the locals would bother breaking in; the majority were rich enough already and surely everybody in Blight knew the Greene's had nothing worth stealing? Also, think about it, the likelihood of some passing housebreaker happening to stumble across a place this isolated was fairly remote. Nevertheless, unable to settle or to set aside such fears, Tea crept from room to room, drawing bolts and securing windows. ("You can never be too careful, isn't that right, Whispers?"). In the low-ceilinged living room the lights appeared to flicker and dip, fluctuating in time to her heart. Maybe she would feel safer if she fetched a kitchen knife? No, no, stop! She was overreacting again, getting jumpy just because she had seen a stray hare in the back garden. None of this was real, she must forget those ridiculous fantasies about Hopscotch being a bad omen. Now, take a deep breath…take a deep breath…

"Tea! Tea! Open up! Let me in!"

Stifling a scream, Tea shrunk back as a frenzied, feral battery of thumps and kicks were launched upon the front door, only feet from where she stood. Initially she was too stunned to process what was happening. She pictured some wounded animal out there; perhaps it had stumbled, disorientated, from the dells of HarmWood, drawn by the houselights. Then, above the noise, she registered the voice. Although raised to a pitch of hysteria completely unfamiliar, it was a voice she could not help but recognise.

"Jack? Is that you?"

Perhaps he was hurt, had been attacked? Tea was surprised to find herself faintly smiling at the prospect. For some reason, the thought instantly soothed her stress levels and strengthened her resolve. However, she still hesitated when it came to opening the door. Even if Jack had been assaulted, what possible reason could he have for being all the way out here in the first place? It didn't make sense; he lived at the opposite end of Blight, on the right side of the tracks. Yet he pleaded so desperately to be admitted that Tea felt she could hardly refuse. Against her better judgement, she inched open the door.

"I need to speak to you!" he blurted out, with head bowed on the doorstep. "I…I…I just really need to speak to you…"

His words were slurred, almost incoherent, as though he was struggling to articulate, which was not like him at all. Obviously Tea had seen him drunk before, but never sloppy, never out of control. Had one of his dodgier friends spiked him with something?

"There were things I shouldn't have said…stuff that happened…" he continued, as though struggling to remember rehearsed lines, lines that had possibly sounded more profound earlier in the evening. Was he trying to apologise? Again, this was out of character. "I know you were thinking about moving away but…please don't. I just…I want you to stay here. With me…"

There would have been a time, not too long ago, when to hear this would have made her so happy, perhaps even to the point of reconsidering 'The Plan'. Yet when they were together Jack had expressed little interest in her, or indeed their, future. On more than one occasion Tea had introduced the idea of moving away, seeking to prise a reaction out of him and, she supposed, secretly hoping he would either urge her to stay or insist on joining her. Unfortunately, every time, the only response elicited had either been a shrug of the shoulders or a lecture on the endless flaws in her plan. It was as if Jack took the suggestion of anybody leaving Blight as a personal insult. So why was he suddenly so eager for her company now? Alcohol, Tea assumed, or whatever else he was on. Most likely he'd spent the day partying with friends in the woods; after all, there were several quiet spots close to The Veil House. Her place was probably the first he had passed on the way home and he'd thought he'd try his luck. Well, she wasn't going to let him in, not after all that had occurred, not even if he gave her that look. Tea was impressed by her own resilience. Although, in her mind, she had acted out a similar scenario many times over, she always half suspected she would falter when faced with the real thing.

"I think you should go home, Jack. It's late…"

"Please…you can't do this to me, Tea. You don't understand what's going on. I…I know who you really are…what you really want. Nobody gets you but me…" Whilst the tone of his voice grew more entreating, almost pathetic, Jack's body language, by contrast, was becoming increasingly aggressive. He appeared tortured, buckled, like he was fighting a disease. "You can't leave…we must…this has to happen…"

Clearly Jack was losing his train of thought, which only seemed to enrage him further. Stopping dead mid-sentence, he tossed his head back to bellow at the moon, causing Tea to wince and recoil. She had never seen him like this, or perhaps just never witnessed this side of him. His words apparently exhausted, Jack turned to Tea with a twisted smile…then launched himself at her. Whether he had meant to hit her or kiss her, she never could tell. However, one thing she could be certain of was that she never raised a hand to him. When he pounced, she automatically took a step back; there was no physical contact whatsoever. And yet, in the blink of an eye, Jack was instantly catapulted several feet backwards, flat out on the lawn, as though propelled by some invisible force. This had the effect of breaking the spell. Jack sat up stiffly, inspecting his grass-stained hands with dazed incomprehension, like a child that has fallen in the playground. Tea herself stood stunned, struck dumb, in the doorway. He must have tripped? Slowly, self-consciously, yet neglecting even a glance in her direction, Jack picked himself up and part staggered, part sauntered away down the drive as if nothing had happened. Tea kept watch until she was sure he was out of sight, before locking the door for a second time that night.

"Oh Whispers, what just happened?" Tea sighed despondently as she sank into the sofa, the cat settling on a cushion beside her. "Was it all my fault?"

She reached for her glass of sherry, suddenly tearful.

Chapter Three: Mr Tender, the Gardener

Tea did not sleep well that night. The confrontation with Jack kept going round in her head, as she replayed and analysed every word, every action, trying to make sense of his motives. Did he have feelings for her after all? In that case, why had he broken it off so abruptly? All through the dark her inner voices echoed especially loud now that she lived alone, filling the far corners of her room, rising to the ceiling. Tea's mum suffered from spates of insomnia herself and could often be heard traipsing up and down the stairs in the small hours or pottering about the kitchen, nocturnal sounds that became comforting if you could not sleep. But, in her absence, everything was so quiet here.

'Quiet like Christmas Night, quiet like my borderline personality disorder...'

Tea allowed a little witch laugh at herself as she adjusted the pillows for the umpteenth time. If only she could switch off her senses yet her hearing was attuned to the slightest disturbance - the murmur of the pipes, the creak of the floorboards as they cooled. And why did the trees keep clawing at her window when there was no hint of a breeze? They are tapping out a secret message for me, she thought drowsily, just like at a séance.

When Tea did eventually drift off she dreamt she lived at The Veil House; the solitary tenant of empty rooms, which by this stage had long fallen victim to the forest. Every inch of living space was choked with grotesque, oversized flora; the tendrils of impossible plants obscuring the windows, serpentine vines creeping across the faded yellow wallpaper.

"I must leave! I can't be late for my driving test!" In her dream, Tea had frantically fought her way through the knotted mesh of roots and thorns to reach the front door. Outside The Veil House she stumbled upon a ring of her childhood friends, many of whom had long moved away, their faces forgotten. They stared at her wide-eyed.

"'It's the ghost!" someone cried, before they all took flight.

"No! Wait, come back…" Tea called out in protest, only to start awake and discover she was talking to herself.

Whispers studied her curiously from an old armchair draped with discarded clothes, where he had bedded down for the evening. Tea found it funny how often she dreamt of The Veil House and stranger still that, even the first time she had dared sneak inside, the rooms felt somehow familiar. The glimmer behind her bedroom curtains told her dawn had broken and when she checked her phone it was nearly half past six; time to get up. It would have been nice to have had a better night's sleep before her big day. She wanted to be alert for both her test and the visit to the clinic but, whatever, she could cope. In fact, she was growing accustomed to dealing with everything by herself. At least she had the day off work, she reasoned as she headed downstairs to fix herself a coffee. Too nervous to eat breakfast, Tea spent the next two hours swatting up on any theory questions she might be asked and running through all the worst-case scenarios she could feasibly encounter on the roads of Blight. In her favour, she surely knew every possible route around the village like the back of her hand, yet it was the pressure, the responsibility that unnerved her, not to mention the ever-watchful eye of her driving instructor. Yes, Robin never failed to make her uncomfortable, the way he studied her too closely through his spectacles, like he was clinically examining a specimen. There again, she supposed she shouldn't take it too personally; other girls had told her they had felt the same. Unfortunately, if you were looking for a local school his self-run company, 'Dewar Driving', was the only option available.

Tea had arranged to meet this Robin fellow a little way down the lane. She would be driving his training vehicle for the duration of the mock as her own car was not exactly in a roadworthy state, the poor thing rusting away in the garage until she could afford the necessary repairs. Never mind; focusing on positive thoughts, Tea stepped out into the early morning sun. She was instantly confronted by the unexpected sight of two ragged figures emerging from the haze that lingered on the front lawn. The first was an older man who hauled a frayed, bulging kit bag over his shoulder whilst pitching himself along on an upturned rake, although he was clearly much too lithe and robust to require a walking stick. A few steps behind him trailed his young ward, who clumsily manoeuvred an outsized wheelbarrow up the drive, piled high with gardening implements. Tea at first assumed this must be a junior employee, as they bore no family resemblance. What both did have in common was they looked weatherworn and a little dishevelled, suggesting that not only were they dressed for outdoor work but they also regularly slept rough in the woods. Any truck or van they had used for transport must have been parked up out of sight, possibly in a lay-by back on the main road or down one of the many dead-end tracks that expired under the trees. Tea was startled by their appearance. It was rare for The Greene's to receive visitors and certainly not visitors like these. They reminded her of a pair of travelling actors from the Middle Ages; like something out of a Shakespeare play.

"Good morning, Miss. Felicity, I believe? Am I right?" It was the older man who did the talking, doffing his tattered hat in an affable manner that reminded Tea of a friendly scarecrow sprung to life. Mystified, she nodded her assent. "My name is Tender, Albert Tender. And this here is my nephew, Elvin…"

The boy hung back awkwardly, lisping some indistinct greeting under his breath yet avoiding eye contact. Perhaps he was uncomfortable around girls of his own age? However, Tea sensed Elvin was not quite as sheepish as he made out; he came across more surly and defiant than shy. And, when she did catch him casting her a brief glance from beneath that mop of raven hair, Tea noticed his green eyes glimmered like Whisper's did when he was watching a bird.

"Your mother hired me to do some work on the garden? Don't tell me she forgot to mention it? Well, ain't that just her to a tee! Mind like a sieve!" laughed Mr Tender, breaking into a broad, crooked grin. "Me and your mother go back years you know…"

"Oh...I'm afraid...she isn't here right now..." stammered Tea.

"That's alright, Miss. She warned me she may not be around at this hour. They're working her to the bone at that place ain't they? What she needs is a holiday..." The gardener took a step forward, his tall, sinewed frame looming over Tea. He smelt of soil and smoke. "But she was keen for us to make a start as soon as we could, like. She said to me 'my daughter will show you in', 'Felicity knows what needs to be done'. That's what she said..."

"Sorry, Mr Tender, what I meant was my mum's gone away for a while. I don't know when she will be back. She's in hospital, she's not very well..."

"I'm sorry to hear that, Miss, but think what a nice surprise she'll have when she gets home..." Mr Tender continued undaunted. Tea could feel herself bending to his will, a force of nature. "The first thing she sets eyes upon will be the most beautiful garden. What woman could ask for more than that, Miss? And, don't worry, I won't ask you to settle up until your mum's back safe and well. Now, if you could just point me and Elvin in the right direction, we'll have a look around. It helps to get a picture in my mind..."

Mr Tender would clearly not be taking 'no' for an answer and Tea really didn't have time to debate. Her mum had been talking for years about hiring a gardener and, yes, perhaps she had mentioned an old friend called Albert who was willing to take on the work at a reduced rate? Aware that Robin would be waiting, impatiently, to start the test, Tea hastily sketched out all the vague, probably impractical schemes her mum had dreamt up for the garden. Mr Tender gave the impression of listening attentively, an amused glint set in his granite eyes. Eager to make her excuses, Tea cut the conversation short by directing the gardener down a side-path that steered through a mass of wilting, top heavy hydrangea bushes until coming out round the back of 'The Burrows'. Mr Tender thanked her kindly, again reassuring her that the garden was in good hands: "You won't even notice we're there!" Striding swiftly onto the path, still using his rake as a staff, he gestured for his nephew to follow. As Elvin pushed the barrow past Tea she thought she heard him mutter something in a low, hoarse voice. Or was he laughing at her? Tea guessed she was just being paranoid. Leaving Mr Tender to work, she hurried down the drive, no longer quite as composed as she had been a few minutes earlier.

Out on the main road there was no sign of the gardener's van, however the test car belonging to 'Dewar Driving' was parked up in the first lay-by.

"Hello, Felicity. That's an interesting dress you are wearing".

It had always been the same, every driving lesson. Robin would inevitably greet her by making some dry, ambiguous observation about her appearance, adjusting his wire rimmed glasses to scrutinize her reaction. Tea could never quite be sure if this was his intention, but of course such a reception immediately made her feel ill at ease, even before she had put the car into gear. There had been gossip among the other girls, who complained to each other about the instructor's attentions but never took the matter further. Her own sister had warned her, tongue in cheek she thought, to beware of men like him with 'reptile eyes'. Apparently Robin did have a wife and young child hidden away somewhere, although they were rarely seen around the village, leading to wild rumours that either he kept them under lock and key or had buried their bodies in the cellar. Tea had tried to give him the benefit of the doubt. Maybe he was just a strange, socially inept, thirtysomething man? Or perhaps his off-putting manner was all part of a personal philosophy, some 'driving school' psychology? Still, she had never warmed to him and could not shake the feeling he secretly enjoyed undermining her confidence in various subtle ways, surely the opposite of what a decent driving instructor should do?

"So sorry I'm late…something unexpected happened…" apologised Tea, flustered and swatting away summer insects as she leaned in at the open car window. "I'm on my own now…I think I said…my mum and my sister aren't around…"

There was a long pause, during which Robin did not respond or make any sign of shifting across from his position in the driving seat. He simply stared up at her, unblinking. Was he assessing the situation, weighing up his options? On occasion in his company Tea had the unsettling feeling that Robin was biding his time, patiently awaiting some undisclosed opportunity. Finally, he broke the silence.

"Perhaps they're trying to tell you something?" he said with a wry smile. "Perhaps they don't really like you?" Again he paused, seeming to savour Tea's disconcerted expression, before adding, without humour or sincerity "No, I'm only joking. Jump in…"

'Rise above it, Tea. One day you'll look back and all this will be nothing' she reminded herself, as the instructor swung open the driver's door.

****

Whether due to female intuition or some extra sensory power, Tea had known she would fail her mock test, just as she had predicted that her sister would pass the real thing first time. Wasn't that the story of her life? She lacked Sea's confidence, it felt as if something was always holding her back. Like any learner, Tea had made a few minor errors along the route, forgetting to check her rear-view mirror or struggling to position during reverse parking. But what had really counted against her was the collision she had almost caused on Kidnapper's Lane, a notorious accident black spot not far from 'The Burrows', where the road tapers beneath a tunnel of trees and remains bedimmed even on the brightest day. Tea had only narrowly avoided a couple of vehicles hurtling in the other direction, necessitating an extended pit-stop to calm her nerves.

If she did not know better she could suspect that Robin had deliberately chosen the most challenging circuit around the village, delighting in her torment as she was forced to take yet another blind bend. However, the real blow wasn't to her self-esteem but to her dreams of escape. Put in simply practical terms, without a driving license she wasn't going anywhere. Robin had stressed, with laboured sensitivity and a barely suppressed smirk, that he would not currently feel confident in putting her forward for the official test. Yet Tea's economic situation would not allow for additional lessons, not to mention the essential work required on that wreck in the garage. Dare she ignore his advice and demand a test regardless? Probably not. On the plus side, at least she would not have to spend any more time with Robin Dewar for a while. Sitting together awkwardly after the test, closer than Tea felt comfortable with, the instructor seemed to relish delivering the bad news a little too much, dwelling in detail over her every mistake. Dropped back on the side of the road, where she had started, Tea considered her next move.

There would be a couple of hours to kill before she could visit the clinic; wasn't lunch hour usually an acceptable visiting time? With nothing else to do she might as well head home and catch up on some household chores. Tea felt like a member of a funeral procession as she marched back up the long drive, her mind mourning the lost possibilities, her anger rising when she thought of how unsupportive her instructor had been throughout her mock. Yes, 'mockery' was the word for it alright. Robin would have known all too well the daunting images Kidnapper's Lane would conjure in the mind of a local like Tea, not only its real-life road casualties but also the legends of phantom hitchhikers and careering, ghostly carriages. No, she must not let her rage overwhelm her, there was nothing she could do to alter events now. 'Time is…time was…time is past' as her mum was so fond of saying. To distract herself, Tea concentrated on the tranquil activity of the surrounding woodland, like the bees at the lavender, so undisturbed and self-contained. 'That is how I should be from now on' she decided as she opened her front door.

To pass the time Tea busied herself with some haphazard housework, hoovering and mopping the floors, making slight rearrangements to the furniture to suit her tastes. It was whilst shifting the sofa that an unusual object dropped out through a tear in the underlining, rolling across the carpet to rest at her feet. What was particularly strange was that Tea had come across an almost identical object when dusting the mantelpiece just the other day, this time secreted inside the workings of the carriage clock. Here again was a small, stoppered glass bottle; a miniature that could be held steady between finger and thumb. Raising it to catch the light from the windows, Tea examined the contents, which appeared to be a crammed assortment of pins, strands of hair and what might be nail clippings, all preserved in an unsavoury, sallow looking liquid. On finding the first bottle she hadn't quite been able to place what it reminded her of, but with this second discovery it came back in a flash. What they resembled were the 'offerings' that mum had encouraged her and Sea to place around their father's grave when they were young. In lieu of any more elaborate, more expensive materials, the sisters would often stuff their bottles with figures assembled from strips of cloth and pipe cleaners, old tights and hair ties. However, Tea could never recall them submerging their creations in putrid water. Then, apparently inexplicably, a deeper memory was triggered. It was another time, long ago, but a similar, queasy sensation. Tea and her sister had found a tatty ragdoll stashed up the chimney and dragged it out to play with. When their mum had caught them she was really mad. "You'll get soot all over the carpet!" she had screamed, snatching the thing out of their hands. Even back then Tea had thought it strange; her mum rarely lost her temper and this time it seemed that, really, she was angry about something entirely different.

Even though she knew they might repulse some people, there was something about the little bottles that Tea found quite attractive and she could not bring herself to throw them away. Instead she made a little display on the kitchen windowsill, where they would become ornaments that, every afternoon, caught the arc of the dying sun. As she pushed aside various condiments to make room, Tea happened to look out into the back garden. Her heart skipped. She spotted faint, concealed movement among the greenery. Oh, of course, the gardener and his nephew.

"It's true what Mr Tender said..." she whispered profoundly to herself. "I didn't notice they were there. I'd forgotten I ever invited them..."

But what exactly were they doing? Tea stood aside from the kitchen window to watch them unseen, from an angle. Although spared only glimpses through the dense weave of wild hawthorn bushes and wizened crab apple trees, from what she could see Mr Tender appeared to be performing some form of ritual deep in the heart of the garden, pacing back and forward as if marking out ley-lines on a map, occasionally bowing down to run his palms over the soil or gently caress the plants. Meanwhile, stood back in the shade, Elvin swayed gently as though in a trance, his lips moving slowly but precisely like he was lost in prayer. Tea shrugged and accepted this sort of work was beyond her understanding. None of the family were exactly green fingered, except for apparently her dad and she presumed, she hoped, her mum wouldn't have hired Mr Tender unless sure he was reliable. Which reminded her, she had more important matters to think about, namely her unscheduled appointment with Dr Chalk.

There was a local bus that should drop her right outside the clinic, the stop only a short walk down the lane. Sweltering heat rose from the tarmac, beating in waves against the bordering hedgerows. A scattering of crickets chirped intolerantly, impatiently in isolation. 'Everything is fermenting' thought Tea, as she felt a familiar, disorderly force surge within her, a sense of unpredictable strength. She never knew when to expect this emotion, and it would always subside just as unexpectedly, but right now she felt prepared for any argument, any resistance she might meet. The bus stop stood, unattended, on a raised verge at the side of the road, reminding Tea of a gibbet. Public transport around this region had been drastically reduced over recent years, the remaining services redirected or constantly rescheduled, so it seemed fitting the stop itself was in such a state of neglect. The wooden post was warped and choked with weeds, the laminated timetable faded, stained by the rain and near impossible to make out. As a child, Tea had enjoyed reading aloud the exotic, vaguely sinister sounding names of the neighbouring villages:

Maiden under Lyme, Cold Slad, Lower Slaughter, Mourne on the Marsh…

Unfortunately, on eventually visiting, none of these places had really lived up, or down, to her romantic ideals. The majority either consisted of a cluster of barns and modest cottages or, by contrast, sprawling estates enclosing expensive, yet seldom occupied, second homes.

Tea waited and waited for a bus to arrive. She had been unable to identify any routes or destinations from the timetable; the print was so old and faint she might as well be attempting to decipher Egyptian hieroglyphics. Yet she was sure, as Sea had seconded, that there used to be a bus that dropped you right outside the clinic. However, here she still was, almost an hour later, stood beside a dead road which had barely seen any traffic since she first arrived. Certainly there had been no buses passing in either direction, only the occasional car in cruise mode, drivers and passengers gawking at her with their windows wound down, derisory sneers set on their faces as if they all knew she was wasting her time but had decided not to tell. Where was Jack when she needed a lift, if he was suddenly so interested again? Forget it; if there was anything to say he could be the one to make the call. Instead Tea chose to text Karmilla. She might have a bright idea and, besides, Tea had promised to contact her with the outcome of her driving test.

'Meet me at The Restoration??? xxx'

Karmilla had responded within minutes. She was good like that, unlike some of Tea's other 'friends' who would make her wait or ghost her completely, pretending their lives were far too exciting to spare the time. The Restoration was Karmilla's favourite pub, although Tea could not for the life of her grasp the reason why. That said, she had to admire her friend's blasé courage and contrary taste. The Restoration was a rough hovel hidden on the edge of the village, largely the haunt of elderly farmers, with cinder blocks for seating and beer barrels or packing crates posing as tables. There was no wi-fi and no lights in the ladies' loo and, following a few double vodkas, Tea would feel even more disorientated than usual; head spinning as though she had fallen backwards through time. Not to suggest that Blight contained any 'cool' pubs as such, yet The Restoration would be the last choice of any self-respecting young person in the local area, even though they never asked for ID. Still, what did anyone else know? Clearly in some unspecified way the place made Karmilla feel at home; she had remained completely oblivious to the open stares they had received from the regulars on their last couple of visits.

'OK! Be there in an hour…xxx' Tea texted eagerly. She supposed the clinic could wait until tomorrow, or maybe she would try and call again this evening. It was not as if her mum's condition was life threatening, was it? She would talk through her options over a couple of drinks.

****

Naturally, the night was never restricted to 'a couple of drinks', even less so if Karmilla were involved.

"It's like I can never leave this village!" laughed Tea bitterly. "I can't drive! I can't even catch a bus!"

"You will! Don't worry so much! I will get you out!" Karmilla announced confidently, slamming down her glass. She had spent the last few hours reassuring and commiserating, patiently waiting for the alcohol to cast its spell of positivity. "You will come and live with me in the city!"

How many times had Tea made a vow to herself to avoid afternoon drinking? No matter how alluring the idea seemed at first it inevitably spiralled out of control. In the back of her mind Tea was aware they were being far too loud for such an enclosed space, setting the world to rights in front of a sparse, shifting crowd that glowered sullenly in the background. Dodsworth the bald, bull-necked landlord threw accusatory glances at them whenever he collected their mounting tally of glasses but knew better than to reprimand his two best customers. Tea was not too concerned about what the rest of the clientele thought. Let them mutter disapprovingly into their beer, it was hardly as if she and Karmilla were saying anything offensive. Nevertheless, there were moments when she tried to lower her voice, suddenly self-conscious in such a small room, concerned that those around them were taking too keen an interest in their conversation. Karmilla would not be so easily subdued, not when she was in full swing, whether undermining Amber's airs and graces ("Who does she think she is, Miss Blondie Princess?") or bragging about the damage she would do to Tea's driving instructor. After a while the logic became impossible to follow, a flow of conversation swirling and returning to pick up discarded leads, yet eventually talk once again turned to the idea that Tea was in some way cursed.

"Maybe our countries have more in common than you think?" suggested Karmilla. "The old women in my village were always talking about hexes and evil eyes and all those crazy things. Maybe Blight has many witches too?"

"Shhh!" cautioned Tea, with a smile. "Don't upset the natives, they might sacrifice me to their Dark Lord! But seriously, it's just run of bad luck, that's all. Don't you ever have phases like that?" Her friend no longer appeared to be listening.

"Witch!" Karmilla turned and hissed across the bar at Dodsworth, before breaking into a cackle. "I was just joking!" The landlord was evidently not amused. He returned what was probably intended as a withering stare, yet made him look more like a petulant, red-faced child.

It was dark when they left The Restoration but Tea did not know the time. There had been no level-headed decision made to call it a day and head home, they had simply run out of money and the bar only took cash. Karmilla lit a cigarette and set off at a confident pace. The smouldering speck guided them like a marsh light, yet at night all the winding, intersecting lanes began to converge and look the same, misleading even seasoned locals like Tea. Strictly, she would not call herself lost, however she was becoming increasingly unsure of her bearings. Also, it was difficult to concentrate with Karmilla insisting on regaling her with tales of vampires and werewolves from her childhood. On a couple of occasions Tea thought she heard footsteps following at a distance and even paused, more than once, to turn and peer into the impenetrable dark behind them. Yet, whenever she motioned for Karmilla to keep quiet, any stalker immediately fell silent too. A few feet up ahead a low, squat grassy mound solidified from the shadows at the side of the road, as though it had been lying in wait for the unwary traveller.

"Ah…Now I know where we are!" exclaimed Tea in a sudden moment of clarity. "We'd better turn back. This is the wrong way, we're leaving the village. Look! That's 'The Gypsy Girl's Grave'!"

"A gypsy girl? In Blight?" snorted Karmilla.

"Well, that's what some people say. As usual, there are lots of different stories…" mused Tea, halting alongside the mound. "Supposedly this 'gypsy girl' who was passing through one summer went missing. Years later they discovered her body down a disused well. Legend has it she was murdered by a wealthy landowner who had become infatuated with her. Oh, or sometimes the dead girl is said to be an acrobat from a travelling circus. And she was found right here with her heart removed. Anyway, once upon a time a woman was killed and her spirit is supposed to haunt this part of the lane. The name I've heard her called most is 'The Lady Outside'. She creeps up behind you as you stand at her grave…"

Tea stopped short and hurriedly looked around, fleetingly convinced that the swift footsteps she had heard trailing them must be those of the ghost. Karmilla did not seem so impressed. "It is probably somebody's dead dog…" she said, causally casting her cigarette butt onto the mound.

Sense of direction restored, Tea steered the pair back towards the crossroads where they had previously parted after evenings out. Karmilla embraced her with drunken enthusiasm and idled off into the night, singing to herself in silhouette. In two days they would get together at the farm and further develop their getaway plans, but not tomorrow as Tea was working her other job at the library.

Typically, at night, Tea would take the long way home along open lanes rather than risk cutting up through the trees. When under the influence, it seemed the safer option. This evening was different, however, for a more pervasive influence infiltrated the summer air. Tea felt a rush of euphoria swell within her, as it often did on her way home after a good night out, only this time it was more overpowering than usual. The summons was irresistible; she must leave the path and enter HarmWood. For, somewhere deep within, beneath the whispering leaves and sighs of a nocturnal breeze, Felicity Greene heard The Veil House calling her name…

Chapter Four: The Library Under Threat

Tea awoke to find her bed full of twigs and leaves, like she had fallen asleep in a bird's nest. For a blissful few seconds she remembered nothing then, in a sudden, spiteful rush of fragmented images, the end of the previous evening came flooding back to her. Feeling slightly hungover and dehydrated, she twisted awkwardly under the duvet. Why did she do it? Once again, Tea had been to The Veil House on her way home. If, the morning after, she would always act as if this was the first and last time such a thing would happen, the reality was that she could not keep away, even though she never ventured inside. The temptation was especially strong when she had been drinking, the way that some people get cravings of a different kind. Last night she had stood there on the path for ages, gazing up at the imposing, doleful façade, torn over whether to enter or just go home. Of course her curiosity won the argument and Tea had settled for a compromise, attempting to make a circuit of the property. The Veil House seemed to grow in the dark, a stately home gone to seed, and Tea had fallen a few times as she scrambled around the perimeters, tripping up stony banks or stumbling into ditches. She must have made enough noise to wake the dead, but out there in HarmWood Tea was sure she was alone. Nobody was following her; not like she had felt back on the lane. 'The Lady Outside' had faded away.

Ah, so her memory hadn't deceived her. There below was the tree growing up through the ruined conservatory. Now if she could just find a way down...

What had she been thinking of? Fortunately, at the final moment, common sense had prevailed and Tea's sense of danger kicked in. There could be anyone squatting in that derelict house; local criminals running county lines or a serial killer returning to inspect and savour his stash of trophies. What proof had she that HarmWood was uninhabited? Clumsily plotting her steps back to the trail, Tea turned swiftly for home, familiar enough with the route to find her way even when walking drunk through utter darkness.

She passed out the instant she reached her bed, as though she had been slipped a poisoned apple. Later, there was a vague recollection of waking long enough to get undressed and crawl under the covers and, at the same moment, imagining in her muddled mind she heard people milling about outside. For some reason she had pictured Mr Tender and Elvin, still labouring in a moonlit garden, but this must have been a vision from a dream, perhaps triggered by her excursion to The Veil House. With sunlight streaming through the gap in the curtains such night thoughts were dispelled; Tea sat up in bed and plucked a stray twig from her hair. There was no time to sleep in, she needed to be at the library by nine and, besides, her BPD symptoms were always aggravated by alcohol. She would not allow herself to lie around brooding over Jack or her driving test. Perhaps it would help to keep a diary of her thoughts, as some mental health experts recommended? Yet the idea that someone might discover her journal decades later, that her words might outlive her, disturbed Tea enough to stop her from starting.

To prove to herself that The Veil House held little significance in her life, Tea made a point of walking the long way into town, down the lanes instead of through the woods. Despite the pints of water and handful of painkillers she had swallowed before leaving she still felt a headache forming, that dull clouding of mood. She just hoped her shift passed more quickly than usual. When applying for the job, Tea had entertained perhaps overly romantic notions of what working in a library would be like. She had envisaged a calming routine carried out among quiet aisles of dusty tomes, interrupted only by engrossing, esoteric discussions with her colleagues as each enthused over their favourite novel. This had not been the case; not in Blight. Depending on the time of day, the floor was either full of shrieking, unruly toddlers or a queue of irritable pensioners asking her to look up absurdly specific items of local history. And, as for her only full-time colleague...

"I'm sorry, why are you asking me? Am I supposed to know everything???"

Tea had received the same terse, hostile response to her first question on her first day, setting a precedent for every interaction that was to follow. Such was the nature of her relationship with her supposed manager, Barb Peeks, whom, in private, Tea had dubbed 'The School Bully', although the woman must have left school at least forty years ago. From the moment they had been introduced, as part of Tea's induction, Barb had behaved as though her new employee had deeply offended her in some way, although Tea was at a loss as to what she could have done. As far as she was aware she had never been uncooperative or insulting towards her manager, not even inadvertently; indeed, she had hardly been given the opportunity. Biting her tongue, Tea put aside the books she had been asking how to label. What was at the root of this apparently instant dislike she had inspired? Was it that Barb felt slighted because she had been given no say in Tea's appointment? The interviews had been conducted off-site by council officials who, strangely enough, must be subservient to Amber's mum, Mrs. Stone. Or perhaps her manager's problem was stress related, the pressure of running a library permanently under threat of closure?

And yet, Barb was perfectly capable of being polite and friendly when it suited her, mainly when greeting the more socially prominent customers it was true, but even toward some other casual staff, leaving Tea no option but to take it personally. In which case, why was she even making excuses for her manager? After all, it was difficult for her too; never knowing her working hours in advance, often only informed at the last-minute which days the library would be opening that week. No, she mustn't blame herself. All evidence pointed to the fact that Barb simply wasn't cut out for management, even though she had seemingly worked at the library forever. For a start, she panicked at the prospect of making even the most minor decision and quickly lost her temper if challenged. "That is no longer my responsibility!" How many times had Tea heard that excuse? It was another of Barb's favourite sayings, used whenever she was abruptly, aggressively delegating another senior level task. Yet, for all her complaints, in her heart Tea appreciated the service to the community the library provided. In theory, it should be one of the good things about Blight.

"Maybe I'm not clever enough, but I like a book that just tells a story, that is what it is. The trouble with you is you is that you read too much into things…"

Barb was rooting disparagingly through a box of new arrivals. Tea wondered why she was so deeply involved with the library when clearly holding the concept of reading in some contempt. Her manager appeared particularly dismissive of any 'funny, foreign sounding' authors and seemed to delight in deliberately mistaking or mispronouncing their names. If Tea dared try and correct her, she would be branded a 'know-it-all'.

Accepting that she was unlikely to receive the adequate guidance or supervision, Tea decided to cut her losses and busy herself as best she could, gathering up a pile of returns to replenish the shelves. She started with the sections towards the rear of the library, if only to gain a few minutes of privacy. In recent weeks, there had been too many occasions where she had turned to find Barb peering over her shoulder, invading her personal space. Unfortunately, the cramped conditions in the library meant they had little chance of evading each other. This was not the rambling, antiquated archive that Tea dreamt of one day working in, but a single-storey post-war build that looked more like a school gym or a job centre, all vinyl-tiled floors and glass panelled walls, gleaming with polish and sunlight. As she was taking her time, stocking the shelves set against the back wall, Tea heard Barb raising her voice and greeting a customer with that forced joviality she adopted whenever addressing someone she considered to be well-connected. Tea parted the books at eye level so that she could take a look without being seen. The new arrival was Mrs Stone, or rather Councillor Stone. She was a frequent visitor to the library, although Tea could not really comprehend why, for surely the family could afford to buy first editions if they so desired. Amber's mum was attractive, thought Tea, in a pale and severe sort of way, that perfect bone structure set hard like she was constantly, covertly, grinding her teeth in rage.

"Oh, Mrs Stone, what a pleasure! My staff and I can never thank you enough for your patronage of our little library. I expect you would like to go to the Restricted Reading Room?"

With an exaggerated display of enthusiasm, Barb directed her influential guest across the library floor, repositioning trolleys and tactlessly elbowing aside less illustrious customers to clear a path. Despite her willingness to neglect most of her managerial duties, the one responsibility Barb was keen to preserve was oversight of who was permitted access to the 'Restricted Reading Room'. Only the most affluent of Blight society appeared eligible to request admission and, as a mere assistant, Tea herself had never been allowed to enter this occult alcove. *What were they doing in there?* Thus far Tea had been reduced to stealing glimpses through the frosted glass windows when nobody else was looking, frustrated that all she could make out were blurred outlines of well stocked bookshelves, separated by what were presumably paintings on the walls. In what she hoped was a subtle ploy, Tea had once even resorted to requesting the keycode outright "just in case I am ever on my own", yet Barb had pretended not to hear. Perhaps all that was required was a little patience. Seeing as her manager had little head for numbers, Tea was almost positive she kept the combination scrawled on a scrap of paper sellotaped inside a drawer at the front desk, although this too was rarely left unlocked. As she ushered Mrs Stone into the reading room, Barb signalled sternly to Tea to stop whatever she was doing and cover the counter, where a couple of customers were lining up. Whenever someone hired time in the Restricted Reading Room Barb would gleefully abandon her position on the floor to simper and serve her esteemed client, waiting on them hand and foot, as though she were a chambermaid and they were royalty.

In quiet spells, with any patrons either reading at tables or browsing the shelves, Tea liked to indulge herself in a favourite work pastime. With Barb still ensconced with Mrs Stone, a privilege that would no doubt be dragged out as long as possible, Tea knew she had time to leaf through the latest intake of books. One in particular had already caught her eye, a glossy coffee table book that reminded her of the sort of collections that had so fascinated her as a child, those miscellanies that were all titled something along the lines of 'Mysteries of the Unexplained'. How she had loved to absorb the supposedly true accounts of hauntings and close encounters, endlessly replaying the scenarios in her mind, wondering how she would react on sighting one of those camera-shy creatures like Bigfoot or The Loch Ness Monster, watching agog as they stumbled into a forest clearing or surfaced, uncoiling, from a local lake. Half the joy had been reading about the beliefs of other cultures and the landscape of distant countries, yet those cases reported on English soil also made her own surroundings seem suddenly magical, like she was living in an unexplored land.

Today's book was entitled, with more specificity than most, 'Green and Unpleasant Land: Witch Cults in the UK', authored by a Mary Machen. Tea was casually flicking back and forth between random pages when one poorly focused black and white photograph arrested her attention. *Isn't that The Veil House?* Tea felt her cheeks flush and she glanced up timidly, as if she feared being caught reading something shameful. The caption beneath labelled the property pictured as 'Blackwood Manor, now in a state of neglect', but on returning a few pages she discovered the supporting chapter to be headed 'The Witches of Blight'. Tea started skim reading at terrific speed, the words blurring, fragmenting before her eyes in her haste to devour the text:

"...evidence of the surprising survival of witch beliefs across the nation, particularly in the more conservative areas of the country...within living memory, rumours of a coven that existed in the outwardly respectable, bucolic village of Blight... allegations of unexplained deaths and disappearances, although no charges were ever brought...suspicion fell upon wealthy recluse Ashton Veil, owner of Blackwood Manor...amid extravagant claims that the self-appointed cult leader was devoted to restoring 'The Old Ways'...had supposedly seduced and recruited a number of influential followers from within the local community... in a curious but fitting coda Veil himself vanished in mysterious circumstances...whilst conducting a blood rite of his own devising, which was seemingly deliberately sabotaged...theories shared

anonymously with this author…that Veil was betrayed by a disenchanted former member of the coven who had grown increasingly concerned by the direction…accusations and resentments that continue to simmer beneath the surface to this day…"

It was all too much for Tea to take in at once. From what she could gather, the events described in the book had taken place in a period fifteen to twenty years in the past. Indeed, she had a light, tingling sensation in the pit of her stomach that suggested some of this material was already familiar. Could these be the bones of stories once known but long buried? Scattered by memory and now difficult to piece together? Perhaps it was true, The Veil House was haunted after all. It was only that the history had been garbled and distorted when passed down through successive generations of school children. Her confusion was accompanied and leavened by a breeze of excitement; the discovery of an adventure beginning in her own back garden. Did 'The Burrows' once belong to Blackwood Manor? Control yourself Tea, she cautioned herself, don't get carried away. It's probably nothing.

"…always a pleasure, Mrs Stone. And if there is anything more you would like me to do, you only have to ask. Your word is my command! No job too small, isn't that right, Felicity?"

Engrossed in her reading, Tea jumped at the sudden presence of Barb who, clearly showing off in front of her eminent visitor, was keen to demonstrate her superb interpersonal skills prior to escorting Mrs Stone to the door. Tea managed a weak smile as she surreptitiously slipped her book into a pile, as though concealing a secret beneath the bedclothes. In response, Mrs Stone regarded her with a regally arched eyebrow and silent glare of disdain. But then, she always looked at Barb in precisely the same way, so at least Tea knew she was not being singled out. Amber's mum did have a point. There was something even more unsettling about Barb Peeks when she was trying to be accommodating, a palpable strain to proceedings, as if she were behaving this way because instructed, rather than through choice. Yet on a morning like this, subdued by a mild hangover, Tea could not face the prospect of any further tension. Hence, when Barb returned to the desk, she wracked her brain for any suitable subject for small talk. Initially, Tea was at a loss. What could she say that Barb might engage with or approve of? But she must act quickly or else risk being on the receiving end of another diatribe about 'the immigrants' or how it was 'best to stick to your own'. Some local topic, perhaps? After a moment's hesitation, Tea decided to share the witchcraft book with her manager.

"Look, there is a chapter all about Blight…" enthused Tea in a tone of innocent wonder, handing over the book, opened at the relevant chapter. "Who could imagine something like that happening here? Do you remember anything about it?"

"Oh, that old story! It was so long ago, must be almost twenty years…" A shade seemed to pass over Barb and she grew tight-lipped, closing the book and gingerly turning it over in her hands, flipping from front to back cover, as if she feared what lay within. "I do remember some silly rumours, some lady writer asking a lot of stupid questions. We told her to mind her business, that it was all a load of old nonsense, but you know these 'know-it-all' types. Machen? Maybe that was her name. Like I said, she was warned…"

Barb trailed off without reading a line; another conversational dead end. She passed the book back to Tea.

"So…where does it belong? At the back, in the folklore section?"

"It would be better off in the children's section!" laughed Barb, who did not often make jokes.

****

Usually Tea would pass her lunch breaks reading in the pokey staff room, but today she was determined to spend that half hour making contact with her mum, no matter what the nurse at the clinic said. On checking her phone, she was surprised to find that Karmilla had not been in touch. This was out of character as usually there would be some update, either a cutting remark about somebody they had met the previous evening or a funny anecdote about something that had happened on her way home. Tea hoped she hadn't upset her friend? In her head, she began running through what she could remember of their conversation at The Restoration. No, no need to panic, Karmilla must just be busy at work, off-line among the strawberries. Feeling more human after a quick bite to eat, Tea stepped out into the enclosed backyard, intent on keeping her personal business secret from the ever-prying Barb.

"As I informed you during your last call, Miss Greene, we're very busy at the moment…" Tea's relief that someone had actually picked up the phone was soon tempered by the resumption of Nurse Hall's defensive, uncooperative attitude. She was adamant that Tea could neither speak with her mother or talk to the doctor. "Dr Chalk does not have the time to contact people with progress reports on individual patients. If there are any significant developments, we will be in touch…"

This time Tea was not prepared to let the nurse hang up on her. Realising pleas for empathy would get her nowhere, Tea doggedly persisted by quoting various procedures and protocol that Sea had briefed her on until, finally, she heard sounds of movement at the other end of the line. A voice sighed "Thank you, Christine…" into the receiver, although whether the tone of exasperation was directed at Tea or Nurse Hall was not apparent.

"Hello, Felicity…" Dr Chalk began wearily. "I understand you would like some news about your mother?"

The doctor proceeded to advise Tea that, unfortunately, there was little change in her mum's condition. She remained largely unresponsive to treatment, under heavy sedation due to an unpredictable, debilitating fever. The clinic had undertaken a series of blood tests, the results of which were expected in about a week. Yet there was good cause for optimism, Dr Chalk assured; the patient had regained consciousness on a couple of occasions and, although still delirious, had managed to communicate a few words on subjects that clearly felt urgent to her. Staff had done their best to interpret her wishes and, from what they could understand, Mrs Greene was particularly adamant that her daughter should stay in the village and take care of the home in her absence. Then there was a name mentioned they were not so sure about. Did Tea know anything about a 'Mr Tender', possibly a new gardener? On the back of that information an agreement was reached to book Tea an extended visitor's appointment in a week's time, although naturally the clinic would contact her sooner if necessary. This appeased Tea to some degree, enough to end the call, which she hoped had not been the doctor's sole intention.

On re-entering the building, even from the rear of the library it could be heard that some kind of commotion had broken out at the counter. The raised voice of an irate, emotional customer was drowning out Barb's ineffectual attempts at being diplomatic. Tea's manager had never been very good at dealing with situations that required complex, sympathetic social skills. For instance, during her first week, Tea had been left on her own to comfort a sobbing customer whose son had recently committed suicide. The tragedy was obviously infamous around the village and the moment Barb had seen the woman approaching she had dashed from the floor, suddenly recalling she had an urgent lunch appointment. Then there had been that incident with the Saturday girl who suffered from anxiety and whom Barb had informed, in public, that it was about time she pulled herself together. As Tea advanced through the aisles it gradually dawned on her that she recognised that raised voice; unfortunately, she was all too well acquainted with what Jack sounded like when he lost his temper.

"Listen to me! I'm telling you I must see Tea right now! If I don't speak to her this minute then there's no point in any of this..."

"Well, I'm sure we can arrange that..." stammered Barb. "But please, Jack, calm down. Think of what your father would say..."

54

"Don't tell me to calm down! Don't you know who I am? Someone like you could never understand how I feel! Tea is the most important thing that has ever happened to me. Without her…my life might as well be over…"

"Jack?" Tea interrupted tentatively, entering his eyeline from among a gathering of curious bystanders. "Shall we go outside?"

"No…it must be here! Now! What I need is… What I need is…"

Again, as had happened at her house the other evening, Jack appeared immediately deflated when confronted by Tea in person, incapable of translating his feelings into words. Not unusual for a boy, Tea supposed, but this seemed somehow different. He was acting as though he were lost in a haze, or perhaps an alcoholic fog, anxiously glancing about as if unsure of his surroundings, handling arbitrary items on the counter as if to convince himself they were real. With a groan, Jack threw his hands up to cover his face, then rubbed hard at his scalp, mumbling incoherently as the crowd watching continued to grow. Then, for a fleeting moment, a light of comprehension flickered in his eyes and a faint smile formed on his lips. Jack rummaged inside his jacket.

"I brought this, for you…" he cooed in a fawning, unfamiliar voice. "It's a present…"

Jack handed across a second-hand paperback, creased and coffee stained, presumably picked out of the bargain bin of the charity shop next door. Confused, Tea stared at him, then looked down at the cover. The book was one she had enjoyed in her early teens, a rather staid vampire romance. It was not the sort of thing she would read now. In fact, she had given away her own copy a few years ago after attempting to re-read it for nostalgia's sake and finding herself gravely disappointed, uncomfortable with both the gender politics and the incredibly poor writing. Why was Jack giving her this now, like he was offering it as some bizarre, misguided love token? Suddenly, a memory came to Tea out of nowhere. When they were much younger, years before they dated and were just classmates, she had given a presentation on the book as part of a school project. Would Jack really remember back that far? Personally, she had been doing all she could to forget.

"That's very sweet of you, Jack, but I don't think I can accept…"

Before Tea could complete her sentence, Jack let out a wail of despair, apparently lucid enough to have registered her bemused, dismayed reaction to his gift. He turned and bolted out through the main doors, scattering display stands in his wake, leaving the library ringing with its routine silence. Tea herself remained stunned, only vaguely aware of Barb dispersing the whispering onlookers, directing them back to the safety of their books. Yet, within seconds, her manager had returned to her side, offering some unenlightened advice on how best to rebuild her relationship with Jack ("You could do worse, Felicity, he comes from a good family…"). When Tea failed to respond to these promptings, Barb pithily suggested that, if Jack had put her in such an unsociable mood, then maybe it would be best for the customers if she took the rest of the afternoon off?

"Perhaps you could get your hair done? You could do with a little touch up…"

Another of Barb's charming traits, shared with Robin the driving instructor, was to constantly make underhand remarks about Tea's appearance. Yet, despite the way her manager always raved about the local salon, Tea never could stand getting her hair cut there. The young couple who ran the business, The Grades, creeped her out, not least because they spent their leisure time performing as a karaoke duo in the bars around Blight. If possible, Tea either trimmed her hair herself or persuaded family members to cut it, although her mum was actually an occasional client of The Grades, having kept an appointment there just prior to falling ill.

Desperately wanting time out, but not anyone touching her hair, Tea accepted Barb's offer and clocked off. She knew her manager was not acting out of kindness but selfishly avoiding having to deal with the emotional meltdown she sensed looming, however today Tea could live with that. Without any real forward planning, she found her steps leading her around the outskirts of the village to the churchyard. Here, on her favourite bench beside her dad's grave, Tea sipped from the quart bottle of whiskey she had picked up on route, driven by the need to self-medicate. Her mind raced uncontrollably, like she was a passenger in a stolen car, bracing herself for the crash that could only end in flames. By now Tea was accustomed to these symptoms. She must wait for the hurt and anger that had been kindled to burn itself out, for they were just elements of her disorder. Yet, when caught up in the heat of the moment, this was easier said than done. There were times when Tea feared her emotions would overwhelm and overpower her, no longer so-called 'quiet' but catapulted, raw and screaming, into the external world. It was her duty to keep it all contained, to hold back the tide, that much she had learnt. This afternoon was just the latest instance; Tea must prevent her unruly impulses from swamping the churchyard, convinced they would shatter the stained-glass windows and fracture the gravestones. Somewhere high above, a branch snapped and plummeted to the ground behind her.

But what really lay behind today? What was the deal with Jack? Had she been so blinded by his sheen of self-confidence and superficial success to overlook that he too struggled with mental health issues? Previously, he had always seemed so sure of himself, the life and soul of the party. Blight was probably to blame. This village was becoming too much. Tea felt like a prisoner. Claustrophobic, trapped; like Maud in 'Uncle Silas' or Emily in 'The Mysteries Of Udolpho'. She took another sip of whiskey and calmed herself by counting to ten a few times over, watching cabbage whites flutter along the hedgerows and studying the shadows as they lengthened, imperceptibly, on the lawn.

After a while, feeling a little more grounded not to mention lightheaded, either due to the afternoon sun or the alcohol, Tea decided it was time to head home. She took the back lanes, entertaining possibilities of escape. There was always higher education? Previously, this option had not really appealed to her; she sensed she was not cut out for university life and, besides, she was not exactly optimistic about next month's exam results. But, anyone could get a place on some sort of degree nowadays, couldn't they? Well, that might be true if you were from a certain background and had the money, so here again lay possible stumbling blocks in her path. As Tea approached home, a couple of hours earlier than expected, it struck her that Mr Tender and Elvin must still be hard at work. She supposed it was only courtesy to say hello and offer them a cup of tea, even if they did make her feel slightly uncomfortable.

Having ignored the pull of The Veil House and walked the sensible route, Tea arrived at her front door. Yet, instead of entering, she skirted round the back of 'The Burrows', surprised by the strength of her curiosity to see how the garden was progressing. On emerging from the path at the side of the house, Tea had expected to stumble upon Mr Tender and his nephew toiling away, yet initially she could find no sign of the pair. They must be lost further back in the sprawl, she surmised. Perhaps only discernible as shadow figures in a dusky grove, or by the trembling foliage as they cleared some snarled thicket, invisible to the eye unless you knew where to look. Just like fairies at the bottom of the garden! Tea chuckled to herself, still feeling a bit tipsy. Then she heard a sound that wiped the smile from her lips and sent a chill through the summer. From the depths of the garden there carried an agonised, strangled cry, like that of a wounded animal. Without a second thought, unable to bear the idea of a creature in pain, Tea plunged into the undergrowth. There was some kind of trouble, she knew...

Chapter Five: Tea in the Garden

This cannot be happening, thought Tea in a momentary panic, I cannot be lost in my own back garden! Yet the once familiar paths were now impossible to follow, turning back on themselves or petering out into cul-de-sacs, each more mazy and misleading than the last. Tea feared that, once dusk fell, she would be unable to find her way home. Already she had lost sight of the house, screened from view by the massed ranks of bramble that had risen behind her the instant she dipped into a depression. Tea was reminded of that caravan park they had visited when she was really young. Bored with her family, she had wandered off to play by herself, only to realise, on her return, she could no longer recognise which caravan was hers. Back then it had been a close, muggy late afternoon just like this one; the same sudden, sickening sense of disorientation. Tea paused to check her bearings and clear her head; those shots of whiskey hadn't exactly helped the situation either. Yet, it was hardly as though there were acres of land attached to 'The Burrows'. Sooner or later she would come up against a perimeter wall or, where there were no boundaries, reach the outer limits of HarmWood.

Again, that plaintive, inhuman whine echoed throughout the wilting garden, sounding like it originated from all directions at once. Tea felt dizzy; sun struck. Perhaps the plants themselves were screaming? Or else prisoners were being tortured below ground, in those tunnels supposedly hollowed out of the earth beneath her? With the tormented wail still ringing in her ears, she attempted to retrace her steps, determined to lay eyes on a recognisable landmark. Whilst battling through the briar Tea tried not to pay too much attention to the alien, oversized flora that fenced her in on either side, the drooping heads of sunflowers that seemed to lean in to leer at her, the banked beds of pansies that radiated vivid yet unnatural colours and released potent, intoxicating scents.

And these were just the ones she could identify. Tea was hardly a horticultural expert yet she had grown accustomed to the flowers that grew in her garden and knew them by sight, if not name. Yet all around her blossomed plants that did not appear to belong to any species she was acquainted with. Was this the work of Mr Tender? But surely even an experienced gardener would struggle to make such a difference in such a short time? And, by the way, where exactly was he? Tea was distracted once again by an anguished howl, this time louder, close at hand. A sharp glint of golden light blinked through the bowers of leaves; persistent, beckoning, as if to guide her. Ah, it must be the sun catching the panes of the greenhouse, registered Tea. Perhaps an animal had crawled inside and cut itself on broken glass?

Now that she knew where she was Tea felt more confident; the garden seemed to fall back into shape. As she approached the greenhouse the sounds lapsed into a guttural, gurgling whimper, as though some creature was striving to stifle the pain and avoid detection. With nobody else in the family expressing much of an interest in gardening, ever since the death of Tea's dad the greenhouse had been left to fall into disrepair, many of the panes within the rotted, wooden frame shattered into jagged spikes. This corner of the garden was rarely visited now. And yet someone had chosen to come here today. Tea watched as a shadow flitted restlessly back and forth behind the opaque glass, frequently ducking down as if to tend to an object on the floor. It was difficult to make out what was going on, for though every other pane was missing these openings were choked with nettles and ivy. Nevertheless, Tea was certain that whatever had been injured had taken shelter inside the greenhouse. But who had beaten her here, also drawn by the harrowing cries? Tea edged her way round towards the front, aware there was no longer any door, leaving the interior exposed to view.

Watching unnoticed, she immediately recognised the lean, unkempt form of Mr Tender, even with his back to her. The gardener was hunched over his nephew, who lay prone on the floor of the greenhouse, his body contorted and convulsing. Elvin appeared to be suffering some type of seizure and it was clearly he who had been emitting those unearthly cries, only now the boy had been reduced to simply gasping for breath, apparently due to an obstruction in his throat, a misshapen swelling that bulged and contracted, reminding Tea of a video she had seen. Yes, that was it, the one with a snake swallowing its prey. Although Mr Tender was attentive to his nephew, attempting to pin down his flailing limbs and calm his more violent vocal outbursts, he seemed in no hurry to seek help. Instead he merely moved aside the upturned plant pots and seedling trays to cradle Elvin in the dirt, whispering what sounded like words of encouragement in his ear, of which only the occasional phrase reached Tea:

"Just let it grow, lad…don't fight what's within you…let the stalk seek the sunlight…"

Elvin moaned and frothed at the mouth, cracked lips parting as if to allow egress, the lump in his throat twisting his neck at an abnormal angle. Tea held back a little while longer, weighing up whether it would be wise to intervene, or if indeed there was anything she could do. Was she witnessing a panic attack, an allergic reaction or something else? Perhaps an untreatable medical condition?

"Such is the nature of 'The Old Ways'…" she thought she overheard the gardener murmur in a nurturing tone.

Mr Tender was evidently intent on delivering a talking cure to his nephew rather than phoning an ambulance, which is what Tea felt was required. She decided it was time to make her presence known and stepped forward.

"Mr Tender! What's the matter with Elvin? Is there anything I can do? Would you like me to call Dr Chalk?"

The gardener leapt up in alarm, as if stung, athletically launching himself from a crouched position on the floor to a stance confronting Tea, landing on his feet like a cat. For a fleeting moment, there was an unguarded, savage look in his steely eyes; a wild beast prepared to defend its territory. Tea could almost see his hackles raised, the hairs standing up along the nape of his neck. Yet, as soon as he had identified the intruder, this expression of hostility crumpled once more into the furrowed, genial mask that Mr Tender always adopted for Tea.

"Ah, Miss Felicity, thank you for your concern but there is really nothing to worry about…" he smiled sadly, nodding back over his shoulder at his nephew, whose spasms had abated to the mild, intermittent shivers of someone struck down by a summer cold. "Poor lad. This happens from time to time. But 'the fits will flit', mark my words. He'll pull out of it soon. Always does. An unfortunate family trait, that's all it is. Inherited from his father's side, I reckon. Now, I'm not up with all the medical jargon but something to do with DNA, I do believe. 'Bad blood' is what many of the folks round here would call it…"

"Oh, I see…" said Tea, although she didn't.

With that she was ushered away from the greenhouse, Mr Tender insisting that he could nurse his nephew back to health, all Elvin needed was a good night's rest. Frankly not in the mood for any further adventures that afternoon, Tea accepted her dismissal and turned to take the simplest route back to the house, a faintly etched dirt track that led through the vegetable patch directly to the back door, with no diversions.

"I think you'll agree the garden is coming along nicely?" Mr Tender shouted after her.

Tea had almost forgotten there were days like this; days when you were relieved to reach home and shut the world out. It took her back to the worst times at school, hurrying from the gates with her head down, slinking down alleys to avoid the crowds. How she had cherished those few hours of reprieve prior to being drawn back into social media; hours spent dreaming alone in her bedroom. Yet, looking back, Tea was proud of her resilience, that she had lived to tell the tale. Things were not so bad nowadays, were they? Slowly, silently over time, she had grown to feel more in control of her life and able to picture herself in various futures; she could also check her phone without a second thought. The afternoon had passed without word from Karmilla, however there were a couple of messages from Sea, mainly asking after their mum. Tea responded with the bad news about her mock driving test, countered by her progress with the clinic, the date and time of her appointment. She decided not to share details of the incidents involving Jack or Elvin, knowing full well what her sister's stance would be: that people in Blight were weird and Tea should move on.

Dr Chalk's gesture of reconciliation placated Sea up to a point, but she still felt his staff had behaved inappropriately and that Nurse Hall in particular should be held to account. With this end in mind, she confessed she had already made the decision to drop in on the clinic herself, if not tomorrow then the day after. Depending on the traffic, Sea's plan was to either drive straight there or, time permitting, make a detour to pick up Tea on route. Pleased that her sister was finally engaging with the family and acknowledging the gravity of the situation, Tea rewarded her with a gushing declaration of gratitude.

"There is no friend like a sister! xxx" Sea replied, making it clear she was signing off.

Early evening was approaching and Whispers was milling around Tea's ankles, wanting attention and waiting to be fed. After seeing to the cat, she made herself a mushroom omelette, one of the few dishes she could cook, watching the dusk as it begun to descend beyond the kitchen window. Peace reigned out there in the back garden, the drama of Elvin's collapse forgotten. Mr Tender had presumably carted off his young nephew to…well, wherever it was they came from. Now that Tea had time to gather her thoughts, the stories of local witchcraft she had read at the library returned to the fore. All afternoon she had been aware of open questions nagging at the back of her mind, begging for attention just like Whispers, although she had ignored the prompting. Was she deliberating prolonging the delight of unwrapping an unexpected gift, or was it more like avoiding opening a letter you dreaded to read? As was customary, Tea's perspective kept swinging from one extreme to another, but she knew from experience she would be unable to relax until she had satisfied her curiosity to at least some degree. Not wishing her research to be disturbed, she carried her laptop up to her room and closed the door.

Tea's first discovery was that the book the library had received was not new. 'Green and Unpleasant Land' had in fact been published fifteen years previously, shortly after the events it documented in Blight had occurred. Out of print for over a decade, the book had only recently been given a low-key re-issue by a small company, which perhaps explained why its appearance had so taken Barb by surprise. Judging by her reaction, most locals must have hoped that the subject matter had been buried for good. In addition, Tea learnt that the author, Mary Machen, had died just prior to publication, the sole fatality in a single vehicle accident. Although questions were raised by the family, any suggestion of foul play or third-party involvement had been ruled out at the inquest. The findings were that Miss Machen, unfamiliar with the isolated country road she was travelling, had simply lost control of the car on a narrow bend. The crash had occurred around midnight on an unlit lane, so visibility was poor. These factors were also used to dismiss the witness statement provided by the driver of the last car to pass the victim, who claimed to have a glimpsed a dark figure rise up suddenly in her backseat.

The empty, untouchable darkness stared blankly back at Tea through her bedroom window and she shivered, involuntarily. It must have been on a lonely night like this that Mary met her death, but that was not the only thing about the accident that was troubling. Was it a coincidence that the author had come off the road on the outskirts of Blight? Presumably she had returned to the area for some final fact checking, to add a few footnotes. Yet, even after all this time, Barb had made no secret of the hostility certain villagers felt towards the book. What if some of those about to be implicated in witchcraft had taken their revenge? Had they put a curse on Mary, melting a wax effigy or hexing a doll made out of her hair? Stop, right there. Tea had to steady herself, concerned that she was throwing herself into unsubstantiated conclusions, simply because they sounded exciting. Wasn't that how all those stupid conspiracy theories got started? No, she must approach this topic calmly, rigorously researching and assessing any evidence, as if she were preparing a history paper for assessment.

However, Tea soon found herself frustrated in her attempts to delve any deeper, and not only due to the unpredictable broadband service, which out here in the sticks was a jinx in itself. For such a potentially scandalous story, containing hints of black magic and suspicious car crashes, there was a distinct scarcity of information on-line. Whereas, if any such thing occurred now, within hours you would be swamped by a tide of shared links, amateur videos and uncensored opinions, all Tea managed to retrieve were a few clunky regional news sites featuring a handful of articles on 'local customs and superstitions'. Tales of fairy changelings upon The Blight Downs and that sort of thing. Although hardly the distant past, Tea was hindered by the events in question having taken place in the days just prior to social media being fully embraced by the mainstream. She sometimes found it difficult to believe that so much recent history had been allowed to pass undocumented, unrecorded; it seemed almost selfish that those present had not thought of sharing. The 'Old Ways' indeed! Yet, in another sense, she supposed this made her task more interesting and enigmatic, like she was a detective hunting down discarded memories.

Long into the night, Tea continued to wade through the electric soup, endlessly clicking and browsing until, eventually, she had dredged up a few morsels of interest. Firstly, a basic obituary for Mary Machen, complimented by a grainy photograph of the wreckage of her car. Also, some scattered columns covering Ashton Veil's occupation of Blackwood Manor, unfortunately none of which included any pictures of the man. Presumably this was because Veil, as the reader was constantly reminded, was a 'mysterious recluse' who 'tightly guarded his past and his privacy'. So, probably not on Instagram then, thought Tea. Of course, there could always be other explanations for the lack of information, as to why there was barely a mention of a witch in Blight. For a start, it was possible that the whole thing was a hoax, invented by the author to drum up interest in her new book. Had Miss Machen merely exaggerated local gossip or appropriated the ideas from other people? Tea had heard some writers will stoop to anything when they are struggling for material. Alternatively, it may be that all the witchcraft rumours were true, and those who feared exposure had done a masterful, ruthless job of suppressing the stories and silencing anyone who dared attempt to spread the word.

"Nothing ever escapes this village…" sighed Tea, as she shut down her laptop. Refusing to be dissuaded, she concluded her best option would be a closer reading of the book. She would borrow it from the library following her next shift.

Perhaps the sound that now caught her attention had been present in the background for ages, but until that moment she had been too preoccupied to notice it. Tea instantly recognised the muffled crying and scratching of a cat, reminding her of when Whispers got shut inside the airing cupboard. The family had scoured the house for hours, trying to work out where the noise was coming from. So, where had the dumb animal got himself stuck this time? Out on the landing, Tea realised the mewling was definitely coming from one of the upstairs rooms and hoped Whispers had not been drinking toilet water again; cue an upsetting vision of him half drowned in the bowl. But no, the rest of the house was so quiet it did not take long for Tea to identify that the cat must be in her mother's room. This struck her as odd. Tea knew she personally had only ventured into that room on a single occasion since her mum had been taken away, making a point of firmly closing the door behind her. One Sunday morning she had been experimenting with a bit of dusting yet had soon grown uneasy at being in there alone. The atmosphere felt like a shrine and her intrusion seemed a bad omen, her presence somehow an acceptance that her mum was not coming back. Since then, the room had been left undisturbed. So how had Whispers pried his way in? Tea supposed he must somehow have clawed open the heavy oak door, only for it to swing shut behind him.

Slipping inside, Tea was a little surprised she was not immediately pounced upon, having expected to be enthusiastically pawed in return for her rescue. Whisper's cries still sounded muted, but neither switching on the light nor looking under the bed yielded any results. As had occurred on her previous visit, Tea began to feel uncomfortable among her mum's things, the specific scents and distinctive displays, yet fought back her urge to retreat. Scanning the room, she noticed the door of the wardrobe was ajar, something which again seemed out of place. The cat had abruptly fallen silent, as if playing a game of hide and seek. Tiptoeing across the floor, Tea drew back the wardrobe door to find Whispers staring up at her, saucer eyes feigning innocence. Automatically, she reached out for the cat but, uncharacteristically, was rejected. Whispers recoiled, preferring to return to gouging away at the base of the wardrobe, where one of the flimsy wooden panels had already been dislodged.

"Oh Whispers, what have you done?" Tea admonished, knowing she would be held responsible for her lack of supervision.

Undeterred, the cat continued to claw tenaciously at the panel, apparently determined to draw attention to the damage. Tea was intrigued and leaned in to get a closer look, dragging aside hanging rows of her mother's clothes, some outfits she loved and others she was not so keen on. Perhaps it was her close proximity to such personal items, the draped cobwebs of chiffon and silk, delicate yet almost suffocating, which prompted the thought to enter Tea's mind:

"Whispers wants to show me something. Mum has asked him to make me see…"

"Life is not a fairy-tale, Tea" she chastised herself, quick to extinguish the fantasy before it caught fire. With hindsight, she had often wondered if her intense absorption in such stories had been early signs of her disorder. Did other kids lose sleep over 'Hansel and Gretel'? Nevertheless, Tea obeyed the irrational impulse and squeezed into the wardrobe as best she could, like a child building a den. Forcing a hand down into the gap that Whispers had forged, she rummaged blindly in the tight space between the underside of the wardrobe and the floorboards. Her fingers fell first on a small object, cold as glass. Awkwardly drawing it out, anxious not to graze her wrists on splintered wood, Tea found she was clutching another of those little bottles she had been unearthing from various nooks and crannies around the house. Until now she had not really given them much thought, considering the collection some secret, eccentric habit of her mother's. Yet tonight, in light of all she had just read, they suddenly took on a new significance. Were these miniature bottles the same 'Witch Bottles' she had stumbled across during her research? Apparently, people used to keep them for protection, concealing these and other objects about the home to ward off malevolent spells and the evil eye. Did this mean her mum believed in witchcraft? *Really?* That might, Tea supposed, account for the mementos on her dad's grave. Now eager for supporting evidence, she thrust her hand back into the hole, urged on by Whisper's unblinking stare.

Shoved further back, as if to avoid Tea's scavenging, there was a bulkier article that required she painstakingly steer it within reach by using her fingertips. This time she did more damage to the structure of the wardrobe hauling her catch out, but hopefully nothing that could not be patched up or disguised later. Reversing out into the room, Tea knelt down and placed the squat tin box on the carpet in front of her, wiping a thin layer of dust from the lid. The exterior gave off a dull sheen, scratched and tarnished, with no engraving or motif to hint at its purpose. Well, it must contain something more important than embroidery, reasoned Tea, or why else would it be locked? Unfortunately, the key was missing and repeated attempts to prise open the lid or force the lock ended in failure. Even Whispers had butted his nose in until gently guided away, nudging at the box as if to flip it over. Tea looked around the room as a clock ticked ominously in the background. If she had a key where would she hide it? Inside a book, maybe, or under the mattress? Perhaps the key had simply slipped out when she was retrieving the box from beneath the wardrobe? However, before she had time to begin the search, in the midst of a casual examination she turned the box upside down. There was a faded, family photograph firmly strapped to the underside. Tea carefully peeled it free from the tape.

The image was slightly out of focus and sun bleached, the way so many childhood photographs seem to be. The setting, typically, was someone's garden on a summer's day, long ago. In the foreground a young woman cradled a swaddled, new-born baby in her arms with a nervous smile that suggested both pride and disbelief. Despite the washed-out colours, Tea instantly recognised the dress as one her mum used to wear. In fact, if she took a rummage right now, she would probably find it lurking at the back of the wardrobe. Whether the baby was her or her sister was impossible to tell yet she was fairly confident she had never met the man who stood beside her mother. Certainly it was not Gary, her dad. The man's features were a little blurred, as though he had been caught backing away from the camera, seeking anonymity under the dappled shade of the trees. Still, Tea found something unprepossessing about his appearance; the smile was more of a smirk and the light failed to reach his eyes. Also, although not particularly striking or impressive in any way, something in his bearing suggested a sense of superiority; the unfounded arrogance of a public-school boy.

Confused as to this man's relationship to her mum, Tea continued to study the vague impression of his face until she thought she felt a recognition stir. An old family friend, that they used to sometimes visit? If so he must have been quite well off, for sneaking into shot in the background was an obscured view of what appeared to be a grand old house. Most definitely this was not 'The Burrows'. If anything, it reminded Tea of The Veil House in better days, a corner of the conservatory that led out into the back garden. But why was this photo attached to the box? Was it a clue to its contents? Whenever Tea manoeuvred the box she heard no sound from inside, no rolling or clattering objects. Papers, perhaps? Financial statements, property deeds, or a will? On the back of the photo, scrawled in barely legible handwriting, so probably her mum's, was written a short sentence:

'The key is in the roots'.

Were these the six magic words that, when spoken aloud, would unlock the box? A sort of middle England equivalent of Ali Baba's 'Open Sesame'? As stupid as it sounded, Tea could not resist giving it a try:

"The…key…is…in…the…roots".

Unsurprisingly, on reciting the assumed incantation, nothing happened. The box stubbornly remained shut, leaving Tea feeling rather foolish, but blaming the whiskey that must still be in her system. Whispers, patience exhausted, cast her a contemptuous glance and stalked towards the bedroom door. Well, if she was meant to take the clue more literally, where did she begin? Outside her house and encircling the village, everywhere she looked she was surrounded by woodland. How was she supposed to recognise the specific tree with a secret in its roots? Would it stand out? Tea sighed in temporary defeat. Perhaps if she were patient, over time it would become clear. But for now, all Tea could do was replace the photograph and return the box to the wardrobe, although she took the 'witch bottle' to add to her collection at the kitchen window. There was no point dwelling on the photo, it probably meant nothing; a meaningless episode of her mum's history, best forgotten. How did that old nursery rhyme go? When they were young, their mum had repeated it so often that Tea and her sister got sick of hearing it:

"Bake it, sieve it, knead it. The past is only what you feed it".

With that excitement laid to rest, Tea crept out onto the front lawn, a little later than intended, weighed down with food and water for Noosha. Having replenished saucers and replaced bowls, she called out into the night, yet her invitation was not accepted. Taking a seat on the doorstep, Tea contemplated the events of the day, wondering if Elvin had recovered and where Jack had gone after he left the library. All of a sudden, the darkness of the garden seemed to fold in on her, pressing down like impending disaster, as though she were lost in a tunnel with a train fast approaching. How dare her mum leave her to face such a crisis alone! This would never have been allowed to happen if it were Sea! Sometimes Tea felt she was not related to either of them! Tea batted away the irrational, intrusive thoughts that flapped around her head like angry crows, a sensation she had experienced, on and off, for as long as she could remember. There was a rustling of hedgerows on the far side of the lawn. Tea glanced up, expecting to see her fox steal forth, only for this image, for an instant, to be replaced by one of Jack prowling the woods, keeping her under surveillance. Nothing. A silhouette moving swiftly away, alerted to her presence. If Noosha were hunting, she would not take her supper for hours. "Time for bed" yawned Tea.

****

As Tea crossed the lawn the next morning she was approached by Mr Tender, who was arriving, unaccompanied, for his shift.

"How is Elvin?" inquired Tea. "Is he at home?

"You could say that..." began the gardener, with a philosophical air.

"With his parents?" continued Tea, who was already late for work and, still rattled by what she had witnessed in the greenhouse, wanted to keep the conversation brief.

"I'm looking after him, Miss. I'm the one what raised him. His mother's never been quite right, see? Not since the day she knew that she was expecting..." Mr Tender explained, pausing between sentences to measure Tea's response, as if teasing her with a confidence trick. "And dad's always been a bit of a mystery, to be honest. None of us could get his name out of my sister. She wouldn't say nothing more than it was someone she met up on The Downs…"

"I didn't think anybody lived out there?" Tea interjected, in spite of herself. She was fascinated by that barren wilderness and its bad reputation. Local children were warned to keep away from The Blight Downs; so easy to lose the path once the mists descended, it was said.

"Oh, some do, Miss, some do…" ruminated the gardener, with a vague, inscrutable grin. "Nobody you would want to meet, mind. But then, my baby sister always was what they call 'a dauntless girl'…"

Obviously content, or amused, to leave the conversation hanging, Mr Tender wished her 'good day' and disappeared down the path beside the house, whistling an old tune to himself. Tea took the hint and rushed to Withers Fruit Farm, accepting that her poor time keeping meant she would be assigned to pick the least profitable patches. There was so much she needed to tell Karmilla, to talk over with her. Usually she would wait to catch her friend at some unspecified point during the day, a lunch break or a chance meeting on one of the dirt paths that partitioned the estate. Yet, today, Tea was in one of those moods where she needed to unburden and could not care less if this was considered oversharing. On collecting her baskets from the packing area at the rear of the shop, she asked which field Karmilla was working in that morning.

"That Polish girl? The one with the weird surname?" scoffed Mick Withers, seemingly astonished that Tea would have the gall to question him about staffing, especially the welfare of some 'foreigner'.

"She's gone. If you are such great friends I'm surprised she didn't tell you. Handed in her notice yesterday, without any warning. Left me short actually, but what do you expect from those sort of people? No sense of loyalty. She left a message on the office phone. Said she was leaving Blight right away. Moving to the city…"

Chapter Six: An Expert in The Field of Blood

Distracted, detached, Tea soldiered on through her morning at the farm, although, really, she was somewhere else the whole time. Beneath the blazing sun festered a darkness within, a hollow space where opposing sides of her personality were at war, draining her with their constant demands for attention. Part of Tea wanted to lash out at Karmilla for abandoning her, believing everything Mick Withers had said. Perhaps it was true? Had she invested too deeply in her relationship with Karmilla and, in becoming too intense too soon, frightened her friend away? After all, it was not as if she had any right to expect long-term commitment. Tea had been aware from the start that Karmilla would not be staying in Blight permanently, that she planned to buy a place with her boyfriend. But then there was that other voice, the one she so seldom listened to but was so often, in the end, proved right. This told Tea to trust her instincts, not the information she had been given. This told her that something was very wrong. Karmilla kept in regular contact, surely she would have at least messaged to say she was moving? In addition to which, Cristian was meant to be in Europe for another month and Tea knew her friend did not have the funds to survive in the city by herself. Am I right to be suspicious, she suddenly checked herself, or have I simply seen too many crime documentaries?

Burdened by these conflicting thoughts, Tea made little effort to inspect the strawberries she was picking, resigned to the fact that everything she touched soon turned sour. By noon she was exhausted; although scarcely half full, today her basket felt like it weighed a ton. Out in the fields temperatures seared and the atmosphere on the farm grew taut, as claustrophobic as a supermarket, with too many people wandering the aisles. In urgent need of some 'me' time, Tea decided to return to the main building and request the rest of the afternoon off. On her meagre wages, she would hardly miss the money. Struggling back along the path with her head down, Tea failed to notice Amber and her friends approaching until it was too late to avoid them. As usual they all looked immaculate, in spite of supposedly toiling away for hours under the sun, their clothing and makeup only slightly altered to suggest a more natural, rustic chic.

"Hey, are you OK?" asked Amber with apparently authentic concern, engaging Tea in earnest eye contact. "Any news on your mum?"

Taken off guard, Tea felt an unexpected rush of guilt over her previous, derisory attitude towards Amber's attempts to befriend her. What if she honestly wanted to repair the damage? Despite their past differences there was no reason for them to continue to dislike each other; school was over and everyone was free to start again. The friends in the background, Dawn Orchard and the three Louise's, were less welcoming and kept their distance, but for once their silence appeared more awkward than antagonistic. Nevertheless, Tea was not quite at the stage where she felt comfortable opening up to Amber about her private life, her caution only increased by the recent confusion over where she stood with Karmilla. Skipping over the details of her mum's illness, she instead resorted to some small talk concerning her nights spent at home with the cat. Tea inwardly cringed as she listened to herself; talk about making yourself sound terminally friendless! Clearly not a lifestyle she could relate to, for a few seconds Amber seemed at a loss as to what to say next.

"Well…" she began hesitantly, almost acting shy. "If you are ever at a loose end, you can always give me a call, OK?"

In all the years Tea had known Amber they had never exchanged numbers, or even remained friends on social media for long. But of course in a small town like Blight you always found you followed, or were followed by, many of the same people, sharing groups and contacts, meaning that if people wanted to get hold of you they would. Not really knowing what to say, Tea smiled meekly and vaguely implied to Amber that meeting up sometime might be a good idea. This peace offering was apparently accepted by all present as, when she turned to leave, Tea was pleased to note she heard nobody laughing behind her back. Handing across her paltry harvest at the desk, she was also surprised that Mick Withers approved her leaving early without fuss, a briefly raised eyebrow the only hint of opposition. Sometimes Tea had to question her judgement of people. She knew she was prone to falling into defensive mode whenever she encountered someone she lacked an obvious connection with, immediately establishing them as an enemy. Maybe Mick, like Amber, was not as bad as she made out, not the petty tyrant he seemed?

As soon as she was outside the gate Tea knew what steps to take. The problem was that she would not be able to relax, or concentrate on work, until she had discovered the truth about Karmilla. Yet her messages last night had gone unanswered, suggesting that either her friend had forgotten to charge the battery or had simply switched her phone off. This left Tea no option but to turn up at Karmilla's flat unannounced, for what if she were sick and unable to let anyone know? Unfortunately, this course of action would mean having to battle her way past Mrs McRogers, the demon landlady who lived on the ground floor and guarded the premises like a gorgon. Notwithstanding her involvement with the local church, Abigail McRogers was notorious for her mean-spirited nature and miserly attitude towards money. Village gossip attributed these failings, at least in part, to the landlady, long divorced, having once been scammed of her life savings by a dubious 'gentleman friend' she met on the internet. However, Tea was not sure this stroke of bad luck quite justified the extortionate rents Mrs McRogers charged for her threadbare properties.

"I'll never be able to afford a place of my own…" sighed Tea, as she approached the end terrace.

Karmilla rented the attic room, which was not equipped with a fire escape, leaving the front door as the only means of access. Tea first rang the appropriate bell, then tried all the other flats, without response. Inevitably, with the racket she was making, she soon summoned up the landlady, who confronted her looking unkempt and agitated, like she had not slept in days. 'I wonder if she was expecting me', thought Tea?

"Sorry to bother you Mrs McRogers but I am worried about my friend, Karmilla, the girl who lives in the attic?"

"You mean that Polish girl?" frowned the landlady. "She's long gone dear, done a moonlight flit. I'm surprised she stayed as long as she did because she never stopped complaining. Quite a little madam she could be too: 'The cooker don't work', 'the bathroom ain't been cleaned', 'the rent's too high'. So I told her straight: 'If you don't like the way I do things, there's nothing stopping you leaving'. That put her in her place and no mistake. I'm not having my authority questioned under my own roof…"

Tea was not persuaded. Something about the story sounded pre-rehearsed, like it had been concocted in the company of others. Nevertheless, she kept her patience in the face of such flippant disregard.

"But when was this? Where did she go? I don't think Karmilla had anywhere else to stay?"

"Seemed to me there was something of the gypsy about that girl…" snorted the landlady with some distaste, perhaps sensing she was being disbelieved. "So she could be anywhere by now. Hang about, I think she might have mentioned something about moving to the city. Best place for her. They blend in better there…"

Without needing to ask, Tea knew she would be refused permission to examine the flat, effectively shutting down that avenue of investigation. However, the hostility with which Mrs McRogers had reacted to her questions supported her hunch that Karmilla had not left Blight of her own accord, that there had been some degree of coercion. Walking away, Tea tried calling her friend one final time but again there was no answer, the connection dead. Perhaps Karmilla had drunkenly dropped her phone whilst stumbling home from the pub, following their recent night out? With this hypothesis in the back of her mind, Tea began to retrace the route to The Restoration, keeping an eye on the grass verges and lofty hedgerows that ran alongside the lanes, just in case they held any clues. As she approached the shortcut that snaked up through the woods, Tea ground to a halt, lost in thought.

What if, for some reason, Karmilla had chosen to follow her that night and met with some accident at The Veil House? The way that you hear of drunken students trailing their friends down to the river, then falling in? Tea quickly dismissed the idea. On a night so still, she was certain she would have heard someone creeping up behind her and, besides, it was in her imagination alone that The Veil House loomed large. For everyone else it was merely a fleeting memory of childhood or, for outsiders like Karmilla, nothing but an empty old ruin. Resuming her course, Tea willed herself to focus on the task at hand. She would not permit herself to picture The Veil House, sitting up there in their shade, waiting patiently like a spider in a web.

For all their secret twists and turns, the tapering lanes that led Tea to the door of The Restoration failed to disclose any evidence of Karmilla's whereabouts. On this particular mid-afternoon she found the pub firmly locked. Dodsworth seemed to open up at completely arbitrary hours during the day, dependent on either his mood or the thirsts of a few dependable regulars. Not wishing to disturb the short-tempered landlord at whatever it was he got up to in his spare time, Tea was about to turn round and head home in defeat, when her attention was drawn to some unusual noises rising from the rear of the pub. Hidden from the road, The Restoration's primary selling point was supposedly its scenic beer garden out back, a small lawn salvaged from the surrounding woodland and decorated with a few picnic benches. Pride of place was taken by a circular pond that glistened in the centre, ringed with bulrushes and weeping willows. Although in theory this sounded picturesque, on her handful of visits Tea had never seen anyone sit outside for long, not even at the height of summer. On one occasion she had accompanied Karmilla onto the lawn for a smoke yet the malign, oppressive mood that clung to the spot, especially at dusk, soon sent them scuttling back into the stale, stuffy atmosphere of the bar. Thinking of that evening, Tea remembered how her eyes had been repeatedly, reluctantly drawn to the pond, as if expecting something to crawl out.

Evidently the garden did not have the same ill effect on everyone, for Tea could hear someone hard at work out there right now. Dragging the pond, by the sound of the grunts and splashes. She scraped open the latch gate with as little noise as possible, not wanting to intrude but desperate for confirmation as to whether anyone had seen Karmilla. Maybe she had returned to The Restoration last night? For a few seconds the landlord remained unaware of Tea's presence, engrossed in the pond as though the sunlit ripples held him in a hypnotic trance. As she watched, Dodsworth used an extended pole to prod mechanically at the water from his position on the bank, either attempting to disperse the algae or perhaps force some obstruction down below the surface. Yet this moment of tranquillity was shattered the moment the landlord caught sight of Tea. Casting aside the pole as if caught red handed, Dodsworth charged towards her, the colour draining from his typically crimson complexion, accentuating what appeared to be a fresh set of scratches drawn across his cheek. The aggression of his advance, the threat of his imposing bulk, pressed Tea back against the gate.

"What are you doing back here? Get out! Can't you see we're closed...?" the landlord screamed in her face with uncontrolled rage. Then, in a flash, he recovered himself, like an actor who had suddenly remembered his lines. Taking a few deep breaths, Dodsworth bent double then slowly raised himself again, his ruddy countenance restored.

"Sorry, I mistook you for someone else..." he offered in stilted apology, before adding "Now, how can I help?" Judging by the pained expression in his eyes, such politeness did not come easy. Meanwhile, in the background, the willows seemed to whisper and rustle with a life of their own, even in the absence of a breeze.

Disregarding her unease at being in a secluded location with a man renowned for his unpredictable moods and who allegedly, even at his age, considered himself a bit of a lothario (a lady-killer?), Tea tried her best to impress the importance of finding Karmilla. Dodsworth responded with something resembling a show of empathy and concern, but she could tell this was only skin deep. Really, all he wanted was to be rid of her. The landlord answered every question she asked, but each with as little elaboration as possible. At first he claimed he could not even recall the last time he had seen Karmilla, until Tea reminded him they had been in the pub only the night before last. Ah yes, now he did remember, but he was certain her friend had not been back since. However, Dodsworth's performance was not quite up to the standard he imagined. His display of innocence was overplayed, suggesting he knew more than he was letting on. Nevertheless, the landlord's non-committal replies soon wore her down and, realising she was getting nowhere, Tea ran out of questions. But all the way home she felt needled, suspecting she had been turned away precisely because she was on the right track and Karmilla's disappearance did have something to do with The Restoration. Tea even pictured Dodsworth rushing to the phone the instant she had left the premises, alerting his co-conspirators. There again, she was conscious these notions might just be the result of her tendency to see deceit in everything. What if the landlord had acted so reserved simply because he had nothing to say?

Returning to 'The Burrows', Tea found Mr Tender absent from the garden. Presumably, understandably, he had taken back some hours so that he could attend to Elvin. Left alone, but considering it best to keep herself occupied, Tea embarked on some further research into those elusive witches of Blight. If it were true a local coven had existed, the members had clearly done a decent job of keeping themselves out of the headlines. Where were the exposés of burnings outside the courthouse, the outrage at some unfortunate being swum in the lake? Tea was slightly concerned her interest was developing into addiction; the quest to uncover more substantial, more graphic evidence just another of her infatuations, an obsession that would burn intensely for a short while before fizzling out. Yet surely this could do no serious harm if it helped take her mind off her mum, and stopped her worrying so much about Karmilla?

Once again Tea's searches failed to unearth anything significant on the shadowy Mr Veil. And the scraps of material she did manage to find, largely relating to the purchase of Blackwood Manor, frequently contradicted each other as to the new owner's personal history. Was he a newcomer to the village? Or was this, in fact, a homecoming? Several sources stated his family were of local stock, but an eccentric clan who lived on the outskirts in near isolation. Tea was not aware of any current inhabitants of Blight who bore that surname, and it was rare for anyone to move away from the village, which was why, at the time, her sister had seemed so courageous. Could it be the family line had died out? From what she read next, Tea concluded that, if this was the case, then it was not necessarily such a bad thing.

Veil's name had unexpectedly cropped up in a selection of science journals, all pre-dating the articles on Blackwood Manor. Concentrating on the paragraphs where his name was highlighted, Tea made every effort to interpret the information, yet the language used in such publications was so archaic and bizarrely structured that it barely passed as English. From what she was able to glean, Veil had once been some kind of an expert in the field of blood. However, his career in academic research had ended in disgrace. Veil had been blacklisted. Struck off registers and expelled from foundations due to his 'extreme views'. Presumably in an effort to protect their own reputations, the academic institutions he was associated with had declined to expand on the precise nature of these 'views', yet the term still caused Tea to shudder. Reading between the lines, Tea gathered Veil's philosophy was something to do with a concept of 'pure blood' which, conveniently, he believed himself to carry. There was an ancient lineage, an 'authentic' heritage that, in his opinion had, in modern life, become neglected or diluted. Veil claimed that, by utilising the proper scientific processes of course, he could identify those blessed with this bloodline and bring them together to reclaim their birth right. The aim was to resurrect a forgotten lore, to re-evaluate 'The Old Ways'.

'the key is in the roots…'

Tea shook her head to disperse the fog of a million competing thoughts. The more she read, the more illogical and unlikely the story seemed. She wondered what Mary Machen had made of it all? As for details of Veil's disappearance, the evidence amounted to little more than a few garbled accounts given by unreliable witnesses. Early that summer's evening, residents on the fringes of HarmWood were said to have been unsettled by the sight of various 'strangely dressed' characters lurking around the lanes at dusk. Some of the more in-depth descriptions referred to robed or hooded forms. When darkness fell, this sense of unease had escalated. There were reports of fires being lit in the woods, the solemn sound of chanting and what may or may not have been a baby, wailing in distress. However, this intelligence only seems to have been shared in statements made after the fact; nobody dared pry at the time. Matters had deteriorated further when, shortly after midnight, those living nearby heard what they mistook for the first rumble of summer thunder, although the storm never broke. Instead this reverberation was followed swiftly by a spate of harrowing screams, seeming to come from a great distance, as though some terror-stricken quarry was being dragged off at height through the trees. Moments later, a band of cowled figures were witnessed fleeing frantically from the woods.

As inconclusive as the resulting investigation had been, the one thing all sources agreed upon was that, after that night, Ashton Veil was never seen again. Blackwood Manor was once again left abandoned. Or was it, wondered Tea? Maybe Veil had secretly continued living there, surrounded by stillness and silence, watching that twisted tree spread slowly across the conservatory and all the while waiting to be called upon by someone like her? Tea scrutinized pixelated photographs of the old house, searching in vain for signs of life but only awakening a haze of indistinct, unidentified memories, as usual. She was finally distracted from the computer screen by a text from Sea. Her sister had not been able to visit the clinic this evening, something had come up at work, but she swore she would call when she was on route tomorrow. Tea sighed and declined to reply. The delay was no surprise and she felt weak and useless for waiting around, as if expecting Sea to rescue them all. So what if their family was falling apart? Tea doubted this ever crossed her sister's mind. She would probably never get here at all.

Tea had already begun preparing for an early night, tidying up around the living room, when she thought she caught a noise from the kitchen. The *thump-thump* sounded like the back door, striking loosely against the frame. Although she did not remember doing so, perhaps she had left it ajar earlier, when stepping out into the garden to look for Mr Tender. Yet, once entering the hallway, Tea knew it was more than just a sound. She felt a presence; a presence in the house. Convinced she was no longer alone, Tea hastily weighed up her options. Did she dare confront the intruder or should she make a run for the front door? There was no point in using her phone. By the time she got any reception out here she would be done for. Whilst still debating the pros and cons in her head, Tea found herself automatically inching down the hall towards the kitchen. Maybe if she took a peek she would be able to assess the situation unobserved, scare off the unsuspecting thief? For once Tea was glad of the poor lighting in 'The Burrows'. She flattened herself against the wall, craning her neck to inspect the kitchen. At first sight it appeared quite empty, bathed in a flickering, fluorescent light that exposed even the dimmest recesses.

But, wait, Tea spotted an almost undetectable movement beneath the kitchen sink, a huddled silhouette that twitched anxiously in the dark alcove among the pipes. Cautious of getting any closer, she clung to the doorframe as she gradually lowered herself to the level of the shadow. Tea could hardly believe what she saw. It was a hare! Hopscotch was in the house! Never before had she seen the animal anywhere but stilled on the perimeters of the back garden, primed to bolt the moment any human approached. But here was Hopscotch, ears alert and eyes wide, fixing her with an ever-vigilant stare that bore deeper than the surrounding darkness. This cannot be a good sign, thought Tea, as she stared back. On previous occasions, Hopscotch had always kept her distance, as though any threat her appearance foretold would be fleeting or remote. Yet her entry into the house, her presence in the very heart of Tea's home, implied that danger was imminent, like a vampire crossing the hearth. Why had she come? Tea

82

felt it was because Hopscotch urgently needed to share some knowledge with her. Perhaps to warn that she too must be prepared, must remain hushed and watchful of everything around her? Lost in the pitch-black pools of Hopscotch's eyes, Tea nearly jumped out of her skin when the hammering started down the other end of the hall. Like a shot, the hare sprung out from under the sink and bounded out through the gap in the door, back into the garden.

Wild blows continued to reign down on the front door. Someone was determined to break in, that much Tea was certain of; the big, bad wolf she had been warned about in childhood. For now, the stout panelling and secure locks apparently presented too much of a challenge, so the assault travelled across the brickwork to the bare windows. Struck repeatedly with force, the panes responded with a dull, pained judder, but Tea knew it would only be a matter of time before they cracked and shattered. All the while, the attack was accompanied by what sounded like a hysterical chorus of shouts and screams, as if a baying mob had gathered outside the house. Above the commotion, the crashes and the caterwauling, Tea could pick out few discernible words, although maybe she heard her name slurred once or twice. If this was the crisis Hopscotch had come to equip her for it was too late, she did not know what to do. Instinctively, Tea grabbed her phone off the living room table and raced upstairs, seeking some degree of safety in the darkness of her bedroom. On her knees, she crawled beneath the window and carefully prised away the hem of the curtain, praying she would not be seen. Her room overlooked the front lawn and out there she could see, not an army as expected, but one lone figure lumbering back and forth across the grass. Every few seconds he would pull himself out of this stupor to hurl himself against the front door or charge at the windows with fists raised. Yet with each successive failure the assailant became more desperate and morose, collapsing on the lawn with howls of despair, before curling up into a foetal position and tearing at his clothes, his skin, in a manic display of self-harm.

Tea knew it was Jack but, bearing in mind his recent behaviour, this was no more reassuring. To think she had once so looked forward to seeing him, spending the morning and night before fantasizing about all the different things they could do. Not that she ever really understood why he was interested in the first place, or had at least feigned interest up to a point. Some evenings even her fantasies would falter, as she was seized with a sudden fear he would see through her, discover what she was really like and decide she was not worth the bother. And yet now, inexplicably, the tables had turned. In the aftermath of their split, how she would have longed to see Jack reduced to the quivering wreck she now witnessed on the lawn; a broken man who was helpless, hopeless without her. Yet, in reality, this first flush of pleasure had faded fast, to be replaced by concern, if not fear. Tea was not sure if Jack had caught sight of her at the bedroom window but, for a second, he seemed to raise his arms to her in a tearful plea for forgiveness, for release. Stomach churning, Tea clutched her phone to her like a baby. What should she do? Call the police? Or would Jack's anger, his fit of madness, eventually extinguish itself, like last time? With renewed conviction, he climbed to his feet and approached the house. Jack had always been a mystery to Tea, but not like this. Once the puzzle had been fun, now she no longer wanted to finish it.

The night seemed to hold its breath in sympathy with Tea, waiting for the barrage to begin again. Throughout the duration of those long, drawn out minutes the silence was broken only by the natural sounds of nocturnal woodland; foxes cried like ghostly infants and an owl hooted from hidden heights. Pressing her face against the glass so that she could see immediately below her, Tea was shocked to find that Jack had disappeared; there was nobody at the front door and the front lawn lay deserted. Then, with a creeping dread, it dawned upon her. He must have gone around the back! And she had left the kitchen door open! Tea hurtled down the stairs and along the hall, catching a glimpse of Whispers bristling under the dining table as she passed the living room. On reaching the kitchen, she gasped and ground to a halt. There was Jack, looking like he had staggered out of a car crash, eyes glazed and unsteady on his feet. Propped up against the doorframe, he pointed an accusatory finger at her, although the words took a while to spit out:

"You…you don't understand what is going on. You don't believe…but…you will. Listen to me…"

Tea could not tolerate Jack mansplaining at the best of times, it was one of his worst and most pronounced traits, but in his current state she found herself actively repulsed by the hostility, the disgust in his voice. Was he now so full of hate because he felt rejected or was this how, underneath, he had felt about her all along? Tonight, Tea was scared of Jack in a way that, for all her anxieties, she never had been before. This was a physical not emotional threat, as though he intended to do her harm, dump her down a well like the so-called 'gypsy girl' of legend. With nowhere left to run, Tea backed up against the wall, desperately scanning the kitchen for a weapon with which to defend herself. Her whole being seethed and simmered as though she were about to burst into flame, like those old photos she had seen of spontaneous combustion. If these were symptoms of her personality disorder, then they were escalating out of control.

Snarling savagely, Jack lunged forward, as if to seize and shake her, the way a dog mauls a toy.

"Leave me alone!" shrieked Tea, sensing something flex inside her mind.

At that moment, the kitchen erupted into chaos. Whether this was due solely to Jack's clumsiness, his uncoordinated attempts to catch hold of her, Tea was initially unclear. All she knew was that they were suddenly under siege, victims of a tornado ripping through the confined space. Catapulted from every direction came a swarm of flying cutlery, a battery of cooking pots and frying pans, all seeming to spring from hooks and shelves of their own accord, spinning and sailing across the room. As Tea looked on, stunned, contents spilled from drawers and cupboards in a torrent, caught up in a whirlwind of china and steel. Jack made a tardy attempt to shield himself, but the damage had already been done; he was bleeding heavily from multiple gashes inflicted by kitchen knives and carving forks. And yet meanwhile, Tea stood unscathed, surrounded by a small oasis of calm, as though protected by some unseen magic circle. Surveying the destruction taking place around her, she felt as if she were in a dream, or watching a film on TV, only faintly aware of the pulsing in her temples and the pounding in her forehead.

Groaning in pain and thrashing his arms about in an ineffectual attempt to ward off the projectiles, Jack floundered back towards the kitchen door. It was then that Mr Tender unexpectedly materialised over his shoulder, a shadow figure looming forth from the garden, observing the scene that greeted him with a grim smile. Catching Jack unawares, he gripped the boy beneath the arms without uttering a word, hoisting him off his feet and hauling him backwards in a bear hug. In an instant, the pair were gone, swallowed up by the night. With their departure, the turmoil immediately subsided. The household objects that had been ricocheting around the room dropped to the floor, lifeless. In the sudden ringing silence, it took Tea a minute to recover herself, to register what had just happened. Why had Jack behaved like such a psycho? And where had Mr Tender sprung from? She dared not even consider who or what had caused her kitchen to come to life. Instead of dwelling on this troubling thought she hurried outside, hoping to catch up with the gardener.

Mr Tender was making determined progress down the side path, dragging his struggling hostage through the gaps in the encroaching laurels and hydrangeas. Lagging a few feet behind, Tea thought she heard whispering carried on the light summer breeze; the gardener issuing harsh reprimands or perhaps even threats. They continued across the front lawn, Tea trailing redundantly in the rear. It became clear that Mr Tender's intention was either to escort Jack to the main road or send him off alone through the woods; releasing him into the wild, like an unwanted pet.

"Please, Mr Tender, don't hurt him…" pleaded Tea, at a loss for anything better to say.

"Don't worry, Miss Felicity, I'll handle this…" the gardener shouted back over his shoulder, panting slightly but not wavering in his path. "He won't be bothering you any more…"

Tea did not recall ever having confided to Mr Tender that Jack had bothered her in the first place, but she understood there was nothing more she could do. It was probably best if she and Jack did not see each other for a while. Returning to the kitchen, she shut the door behind her and picked up a broom. Tea was confronted with a scene of devastation; windowpanes cracked, cupboard doors hanging off their hinges and tiles littered with broken dinner plates and mangled utensils. Even her burgeoning collection of 'witch bottles' had been shattered, leaking a foul-smelling liquid across the floor. Holding her nose, Tea swept up the shards of glass and matted contents, hastily depositing them in the bin.

Chapter Seven: Jack-In-The-Green

Blue light, too brash to be mistaken for moonlight, swept through the curtains and streaked across the ceiling. Her bedroom briefly illuminated, Tea stirred restlessly beneath the covers, uncertain as to whether she was still dreaming. Following her cursory attempt to clean up the kitchen she had drifted about downstairs for a while, half expecting something else to happen. Yet she had seen no more of Jack or Mr Tender that evening; presumably tempers had cooled and both had skulked home to sleep it off. Unfortunately, Tea had not found it quite so easy to relax. All through the night she had been disturbed by activity that carried from the main road, heavy traffic and raised voices and now these flashing blue lights that filtered through the gaps in the trees. Initially, in her drowsy state, Tea had dismissed the intrusions as part of her dream, which was something to do with flying saucers and search parties in the woods. However, as her mind cleared, it became apparent that this must be the Emergency Services responding to yet another accident. Sadly, they were regular occurrences around here. Too many locals had become blasé about driving under the influence, assured they were unlikely to encounter anybody along the back lanes as they sped home from an outlying pub. But, of course, all it took was one unforeseen pedestrian, one sharp bend too many down Kidnapper's Lane. Tea wondered if Mary Machen had been sober when she had her crash? She was a writer after all.

Sure enough, early next morning when Tea left for work, down the far end of the lane she could see a section was cordoned off with security tape and traffic cones, a lone police officer standing guard. But she had more pressing concerns this morning, in fact a tidal wave of worries seemed to be bearing down on her. As she rambled into town, straying from open roads into unfrequented footpaths, Tea spent time wrestling with her problems, crossing them off the list wherever she could. There was no question her relationship with Jack had reached the end of the line, an admission that affected her less than expected; the emphasis was now on him to sort himself out and make amends. And, if Sea could get her act together, hopefully by this evening the sisters should have a better idea of their mum's prognosis. As for Karmilla, Tea braced herself to face a familiar pain. Unaccountable as it was, she suspected she would have to accept her best friend's departure and the likelihood they would never see each other again. Tea supposed she would survive. It would not exactly be the first time she had experienced the abrupt termination of a friendship, an intimacy dissolving into an absence, an inexplicable silence. Perhaps this was to be the pattern for the rest of her life?

Then there were the rogue thoughts she really dared not confront yet; absurd ideas that she was in some way responsible for that eruption in the kitchen last night. Sensing the storm clouds gathering inside her head, Tea fought to dispel them by concentrating on the tasks awaiting her at the library. It must be the change in the weather oppressing her mood, she concluded; the sky a little overcast following an extended spell of unbroken sunshine.

As was the case every day, there were some basic preparations to be carried out before the library could open to the public. Since starting work here, Tea had become reconciled to undertaking these duties alone, clearing the aisles and rearranging the displays whilst Barb dawdled over her tea and toast in the kitchen. However, this morning she intended to turn this lack of support to her advantage. Tea was set upon borrowing their copy of 'Green and Unpleasant Land' and, although she could not really explain why, her instincts told her to keep this hidden from Barb Peeks. So, with the shelves stocked and a few minutes to spare, Tea slipped unseen towards the 'Folklore' section. However unreliable some considered her research, Mary Machen must surely be able to shed at least a little light on Ashton Veil and Blackwood Manor. Yet Tea's heart sank to discover the book was no longer where she had placed it, slotted in slightly out of order so that only she would know where to look. A quick flick through 'Local History' and a search of the trolleys, where her manager usually deposited titles she did not know how to deal with, also yielded nothing. They had such a limited clientele these days, Tea thought it unlikely the book would be on loan already. So why had it disappeared?

Could Barb have reallocated the book to the Restricted Reading Room in some petty move to prevent Tea reading it? Naturally Tea tried the door, as she did most days when unobserved, only to discover it locked, as always.

Accessing the electronic records at the desk only added to the mystery. Tea could find no record of the library ever having received the book, yet she was certain she had scanned it into the system on arrival. 'Green and Unpleasant Land' appeared to have been wiped from their records, as though it had never existed. Had Blight resorted to burning books, sighed Tea in exasperation? Perhaps her manager had alerted authorities to the receipt of a forbidden text? Out of time, Tea had to admit defeat. There was no other choice, she would have to ask Barb if she knew where the book was...

"I'm sorry, why are you asking me? Am I supposed to know everything???"

Well, Tea supposed she should have seen that coming; she could have kicked herself for even deigning to make the effort. Overlooking her manager's habitual rudeness, she put the missing book to the back of her mind and immersed herself in the work routine. There was the usual, regular parade of 'interesting' characters through the library, some of whom Tea liked but many of which, contrary to Barb's insistence, she found more offensive than 'eccentric'. Yet every time she reshuffled the shelves or updated the database she knew she was subconsciously searching for Mary Machen's misplaced book, like when she used to root through the stock of second hand book shops as a child, hoping to find something by her favourite authors. Sadly, this morning, Tea was out of luck.

Aside from her secret quest, nothing else appeared out of the ordinary, albeit that Barb was receiving an inordinate amount of phone calls. Some of these were apparently personal, and she would scurry from the floor before answering. Yet she was also taking calls at the counter, something she typically went out of her way to avoid, even when at her most amenable. How Tea would squirm in discomfort on the rare occasion her manager did pick up the phone, forced to listen to her snap and sigh wearily at perfectly reasonable questions from service users. So why was Barb being so hospitable today? It was as though she were awaiting some urgent message or was required to intercept some important news. Problems at home? Or perhaps her manager was merely indulging one of her more valued clients? Mrs Stone, for example?

It was not until late afternoon, with Tea already mentally in her coat and halfway out the door, that it became apparent there was some sort of disturbance on the street outside. Customers glanced up from the books and began to gravitate towards the glass front of the building, drawn by the muffled sound of a crowd. Tea was equally as curious, intrigued by the possibility that something dramatic might be occurring on a dull Friday afternoon in Blight. However, as she hurried from the aisle she noticed, out of the corner of her eye, that Barb was resisting the tide, retreating into the Restricted Reading Room. This seemed out of character for someone so often found peering over your shoulder and, later, Tea would come to suspect that Barb had somehow been given advance warning of what was brewing out on the pavement.

"What's going on? What shall we do?" asked Tea, approaching her manager.

"That is no longer my responsibility!" announced Barb in a tone of scarcely controlled panic, briskly departing the floor.

Now the sole member of staff in attendance, the throng of library patrons parted to provide Tea with a direct path to the windows, looking to her with questioning expressions, as if she alone could quell the commotion gathering force outside. A huddled circle had congregated on the pavement, mainly consisting of people Tea knew from school. In different circumstances, she would simply have assumed this was another social event she had not been invited to; excluded from a group chat, texts ignored. Yet the scene before her bore more the atmosphere of a solemn vigil than an impromptu party. Every face was struck numb with shock, some of the boys sporadically breaking into disbelieving grins, whilst a few of the girls pressed fingers to the bridges of their nose, eyes brimming with tears. And, there in the midst of them all, was Amber Stone, wailing like a banshee. That was when Tea realised there was something seriously wrong. There was no way Amber would ever allow herself to appear in public in such a state, clothes clearly thrown on without a thought and makeup running down her face. No, not unless something truly terrible had happened. A hollow sensation gnawing at her belly, Tea saw herself sleepwalk through the library door, needing to know what everyone was talking about yet dreading what she might hear. As soon as she stepped out onto the street, she caught Amber's attention:

"This is all your fault!" screamed Amber in a frenzy, pushing aside her stunned peers to square up to Tea. "None of this would have happened if it wasn't for you!"

"But Amber I…" faltered Tea, scared and confused. She had never seen Amber like this before. Sure, she could be spiteful, but she never lost her poise. "Amber…I don't understand. What have I done?"

"Jack is dead! Jack is dead because of you!"

****

For some time after the event, Tea would struggle to piece together the rest of that afternoon. All she could recall was a sequence of disparate images that impacted on her like startling, distinct moments from a dream. Or, to be more precise, a nightmare. There was Amber sobbing uncontrollably, too distraught to strike Tea, which is what most spectators seemed to have been anticipating. Then, from nowhere, the sudden appearance of Mrs Stone, asserting her authority to disperse the crowd. In an awkward display of maternal concern, she had wrapped protective arms around Amber and guided her away, announcing to all present, as much as to her daughter:

"This is not helping. This won't turn back the clock..."

And, cowering in the library entrance, Barb Peeks had chimed in:

"Quite right, Mrs Stone! I'm so glad we think alike!"

A merry-go-round of invasive, distorted faces whirled around Tea, deafening her with their baying and whooping; for a minute, it felt as if she had been dragged back to the school playground. Later, she had a vague memory of being escorted into the relative calm of the library by somebody who had designated themselves her primary carer. It was Sarah from the Baptist Church, who Tea had briefly befriended in The Brownies, until she had got fed up with her 'borrowing' things that never got returned. Without being asked, Sarah had launched into a garbled but prolonged account of Jack's demise, not thinking to spare Tea the gruesome details. The scene of the accident had been the stretch of road, not far from 'The Burrows', that Tea had seen cordoned off first thing this morning.

"They say the driver didn't see him until it was too late..." enthused Sarah, seeming to relish her role as the bearer of bad news. "Apparently Jack was acting crazy! Like he was possessed! It looked as if he deliberately ran at the headlights. The car had no time to swerve or slow down..."

How she had managed to extricate herself from Sarah and the library was a mystery. Yet by dusk Tea had absconded to once more traipse the isolated, untended country lanes; something she felt like she had been doing half her life. Her original impulse had been to seek sanctuary in the churchyard, but she could no longer feel at peace there knowing that Jack would soon be joining the others who were laid to rest. Under the earth, in the green. Hence Tea changed course, wandering aimlessly out into the fields, following worn out paths to places even she was a stranger to, or had at least forgotten about over the years. She wept on the banks of a lonely mill pond and mourned among the ruins of unknown buildings, cursing herself for her mistreatment, her misjudgement of Jack. Already, it was the good memories that held sway over her imagination, obscuring the breakups and the bad times.

For a while Tea was driven only by an urge to keep on walking, she supposed hoping that once she crossed the boundaries of Blight she would leave all the hurt behind. But, seriously, who was she kidding? There was no escape. She was trapped here, abandoned by family and friends alike. And now, with that first acid rush of adrenalin depleted, all Tea wanted to do was to hide from the world. As darkness fell, she found a secluded spot in the woods and curled up in a foetal position. Despite her predicament, Tea could not help but laugh bitterly at herself. Who did she think she was? She had become a cliché, a stereotype - the weeping woman of folklore; a windswept, persecuted Bronte heroine. Yet this realisation only compounded her sorrow; it was no comfort knowing that people had suffered the same pain over centuries and the world was still without a cure.

And all the time Amber's accusations hounded her conscience. It was true. It *was* her fault. If Jack had not been at 'The Burrows', if she had not sent him away, he would never have been alone on the lane so late at night. But hadn't Mr Tender said he would take care of things? Why had the gardener let someone, in such an obviously vulnerable state, run off by themselves? Had they had a fight? Perhaps Mr Tender was more directly involved than suspected? Could he have shoved the incapacitated Jack, accidentally or not, into the path of the oncoming vehicle? No, flinched Tea, surely that was a leap too far?

Distant church bells interrupted her train of thought, banishing some of her fears back to fairyland. Tea soon lost count of the chimes but, with her anguish temporarily exhausted, she grew suddenly ashamed by her behaviour. Picking herself up off the rapidly cooling grass, she wiped the tearstains from her cheeks and brushed the woodland debris from her clothes. What alternative was there but to swallow her pride and return home, pretend nothing had happened? It was all very well to fantasize about leaving her hometown but, deep down, a sixth sense told her that, should the opportunity arise, something would always stop her from going. Formerly, Tea might have accused herself of inventing excuses, be persuaded that she was placing unnecessary obstacles in her path to mask her own lack of resolve. But now, considering the way recent events had unfolded, she could almost believe that it was some external force keeping her under curfew, restricting her movements. With this conspiracy theory running around her head, Tea retraced her route along trails and bridleways that had grown even more unfamiliar under moonlight. Unsteady on her feet, she stretched out her arms to maintain her balance. If any passing stranger had happened to catch sight of Tea at that moment, had crossed her path in that nocturnal wilderness, they might be forgiven for fleeing in fright, having mistaken her for a living dead girl. Stumbling upon solid ground, Tea at last recognised her whereabouts. She had surfaced within the shadow of Gibbet Hill, which meant that this must be Black Dog Lane.

On approaching 'The Burrows', half an hour later, Tea could hear the phone ringing on the other side of the front door, echoing along the empty hallway. This was a rare occurrence and she hurried for her keys. Hardly anyone used the landline anymore, especially at night. Perhaps it was an urgent call from the clinic? By the time Tea had made it inside the phone had fallen silent, but only for a matter of seconds. The shrill peal started up again before she even had a chance to take her shoes off. Tea lunged for the receiver, to be greeted by the last person she expected. On the other end of the line was Amber.

"Hi…Tea, it's me. I just wanted to apologise for what I said, the way I behaved earlier. I was totally out of order…"

"Oh…right…that's OK. I guess we're all a little messed up right now…" Although Amber sounded genuinely repentant, Tea was not in the mood to speak to anyone. Certainly not about Jack.

"Yeah, well, that's what I wanted to talk to you about…" continued Amber in a frail voice, drained of her usual self-assurance. "Obviously, it's The Summer Fayre tomorrow and they aren't going to cancel it, not just because of…what has happened. But some of us thought maybe we could turn the day into a sort of remembrance service for Jack? I was thinking of doing a speech and we can all film our own tributes for a memorial site? Perhaps a candlelit vigil later? I haven't had time to figure out the details yet. What do you think? Before you say anything, I know it might not sound like the sort of thing you would usually be into but…it might help? People I talked to…we all agreed it would be a good for you to be there?"

"The Fayre? Fine…I'll think it over…" conceded Tea, after an awkward, unintentional pause. She had completely forgotten about Blight's 'High Summer Fayre', even though they held it every year on the village green. A 'traditional' selection of stalls, games and music curated by local dignitaries, Mrs Stone among them. Amber was right. it was the kind of event Tea had outgrown and would typically avoid at all costs. In the present circumstances, she felt less inclined to attend than ever. But anything to get Amber off the phone. "Thanks for calling. I'll…I'll try and be there…"

"Sure, no worries Tea. It's not like you have to decide tonight…" To be fair to Amber, she sounded as eager to end the conversation as Tea was. In the short time they had been speaking her tone had grown increasingly strained and uncertain, as though she were being made to say things against her will. "Well…hopefully we'll catch up tomorrow? And Tea…sorry. About everything…"

In spite of the apologies, the phone call did not raise Tea's spirits. It rattled her that Amber had taken the responsibility for organising anything concerning Jack; she was quite capable of holding a service by herself. And why was she, the ex-girlfriend, who ostensibly knew Jack better than anyone, receiving invites from somebody who was supposedly no more than a school friend? But that was all too much to dwell upon. What Tea really needed this evening was a sympathetic listener. On checking her phone, she noticed she had missed several calls from her sister. Sea must have been attempting to contact her whilst she was out of range of a signal, having her meltdown in the middle of nowhere. Requiring some privacy, Tea made a quick circuit of the grounds to ensure that Mr Tender really had gone home. Of course, there was no earthly reason he should still be haunting the garden at this hour, but then why had he been on the premises so late last night? As grateful as she had been for his intervention with Jack, it made no sense to Tea. What had delayed him so long? What had he been doing out there? Fortunately, Tea was able to satisfy herself that Mr Tender was absent this evening, the garden having been left to settle into its accustomed, soporific stirrings.

"It may not seem like it now, Tea, but it will get better…"

Tea could hardly contain her relief when, for once, her sister had picked up immediately. Overwhelmed by intense emotions that had been bottled up far too long, she immediately launched into a tearful outpouring of everything that occurred in the last twenty-four hours, from her confrontation with Jack in the kitchen to hearing of his untimely death. This revelation understandably caught Sea off guard; she had been expecting something much more mundane, the sort of humdrum relationship headaches that people confided to her on a daily basis. Tea knew she had put her sister on the spot and was impressed by how quickly she adjusted to news of a genuine tragedy, comforting and consoling as best she could. If there was little to be said beyond the standard 'there was nothing you could do' or 'it will get better' then Sea managed to tailor the words to the needs of her sibling, wrapping things in cotton wool where appropriate.

'Sometimes you need to share such things with a sister' thought Tea. 'And that is what I have been missing. If only I could find more sisters…'

However, tonight there was so much to speak of they could not restrict their conversation to Jack alone. Adopting some old, familiar tricks she used to deal with her BPD, Tea was gradually able to steady herself, soothing her mind and breathing more easily. When she was in a position to move on, she asked after their mum. Sea explained that she had visited the clinic that afternoon, as promised, but was now back at home.

"I did try to call you at the library this morning, but that woman you work with told me you'd taken the day off…"

This was not difficult to believe. Barb had been behaving strangely all day, exceptionally brittle even for her, leaving Tea walking on eggshells. Also, she had insisted on intercepting all the telephone enquiries, which was uncharacteristically generous. But why did Barb not pass on the message? Why would she want to prevent the sisters from talking? Although her manager had claimed in the past to have a poor memory, Tea had always suspected it was more selective, a ruse introduced to avoid any task she did not want to undertake.

"Anyway…" resumed Sea "I reached the clinic about two in the afternoon and straight away I could tell that something wasn't right. I just had that feeling, you know, like your shadow is tapping you on the shoulder. At first I was glad to get inside. These places are always so air conditioned and it was hot as hell walking across the car park. But the atmosphere in Dr Chalk's felt somehow unfriendly. I mean, even more unwelcoming than most clinics or hospitals. There were pot plants around reception and paintings on the walls, but the light seemed dimmer than usual and the corridors smelt of this weird, sickly-sweet antiseptic, almost like incense. So, as you can probably tell, I was already on edge before I said a word to the desk clerk. Then, when I asked, she told me nobody had been admitted under mum's name! It's not that big a place! It's a private clinic on a new estate. How many patients can they have? Well, what was I supposed to do? Of course I caused enough of a scene to persuade this poor girl, who looked totally confused, to go and check with someone more senior. I assumed she would be back in, like, two minutes. But, seriously, I was left waiting there alone for half an hour. No sign of any other visitors or staff, deathly silent. That was when my Nancy Drew instinct kicked in. I decided I would do a bit of investigating by myself, just to get an idea of what was really going on behind the scenes. Not that my detective work was exactly an instant success. I didn't have a clue where I was going so I wandered the corridors opening doors at random, just to see what was behind them. It's not as if there was anyone to stop me. But all I discovered were bedridden patients in single rooms, lying alone with the curtains drawn. Most of them were out like a light, but a few woke up when I entered…"

"Oh my God, Sea! What were you doing??? What did they say???"

"They didn't really say anything, just stared, confused. I swear some of them gave me this look, like they were pleading. But, I didn't give them much thought, to be honest. My main concern was to find mum. Now, where was I? Oh, yeah. In the next fifteen minutes I must have searched half the building, even the stairwells. By then I realised I was probably trespassing and would end up getting arrested for no good reason. So I tried to find my way back to reception, only I must have taken a wrong turn. I finished up in this loading bay out the back. At least I found a member of staff there, a porter on a cigarette break. This guy looked a bit flustered when I approached him. I'm not sure whether due to being caught taking a crafty fag break or because I was female. I don't know why, I just got the impression that he didn't talk to many women. At this stage, I guess it might have helped to tell the truth, right? But I couldn't stop myself! The next thing I knew I was making up some ridiculous story about a dying aunt who needed me at her bedside before it was too late. Did he know where I could find her? The porter, Dunstan, acted a bit wary at first but, Tea, how could he resist this damsel in distress? Eventually I coaxed out of him that maybe the lady I was looking for was the one kept under observation in the 'Isolation Unit'…"

"That doesn't sound good…" Despite the wry understatement, Tea heard her voice waver.

"Yeah, I was pretty shocked when he said that, but I think I hid it well. Then this Dunstan directs me across the yard to a row of small, red brick shelters that looked like they belonged on an army base. He pointed out one in the middle and I wondered if he was having me on. It didn't look very medical. But I figured I had bothered Dunstan enough and I didn't want to get the guy in trouble. In fact, he seemed glad to get back inside. The front door of the shelter was locked so I had to slip down the side to find a window. The window clearly hadn't been washed in ages and was all clouded over, plus there wasn't a lot of room to manoeuvre with the hut next door being so close, but I pressed my face up against the glass to get a better look. And, Tea, it was not easy to see, but I know it was mum locked up in there! Initially, I thought the patient was asleep, but she must have recognised my shadow at the window because she struggled up among the sheets and stretched out an arm towards me. I didn't know what to do! All I could think of was rescuing her somehow! So I ran round to the front but the door still wouldn't budge. There I was wrestling with the handle when this Nurse Hall suddenly appeared behind me…"

"That's the nurse I warned you about!" yelled Tea. "The one who always makes me feel like I have ruined her day if I dare ask a question…"

"Well, she isn't any more charming in the flesh" smirked Sea, curling her lip at the other end of the line. "She made me think of that wallpaper we used to have as kids. The one with The Witch trying to tempt Snow White with a poison apple? That's who Nurse Hall reminded me of. Not Snow White, the other one…"

"What did she say about mum? About keeping her prisoner?"

"Obviously I took her to task over it right there and then…" seethed Sea, her anger still raw. "How could they keep their patients confined like that? What right had they to keep mum isolated from her family? All that stuff…And the weird thing was, she didn't actually deny anything. The woman seemed totally out of her depth, like she couldn't really handle the authority she'd been given. Her only defence was to stare daggers at me whilst mumbling some vague excuses about mum possibly being infectious, a danger to other patients, etcetera. Yet, when I asked, she couldn't even say what the diagnosis was! So I made it understood this was not acceptable and that I was going to have mum transferred to the NHS hospital where I work. You would be happy with that, right, sis? It makes sense to me…"

"One hundred percent" affirmed Tea. "I didn't want her shipped off to that clinic in the first place. We couldn't really afford the fees, but I was bullied into it. Nobody round here seems to have a clue what they actually do? And, besides, I've never trusted that Dr Chalk. He gives me the creeps…"

"Funnily enough, that's exactly who I was referred to. When it became apparent that this Nurse Hall couldn't string a coherent argument together, she played the get-out card by directing me to Dr Chalk. Apparently he was 'busy' but I demanded I be made an appointment with him tomorrow, to discuss the transfer. In the meantime, I was escorted from the premises by a couple of burly security guards, Nurse Hall still insisting mum was in no condition to receive visitors. There didn't seem any point in arguing it further. End of story is I'll make enquiries at my hospital in the morning and agree arrangements. Then I'll head back to the clinic in the afternoon and persuade Dr Chalk to sign over responsibility for mum's care. You never know, she might even be discharged? It makes me so mad, Tea! Wait till I see Dr Chalk tomorrow! Thinks he can do what he likes because of his money and status. But he won't silence me!"

"OK, well, will you let me know what is happening?" requested Tea meekly, always reluctant to push too many demands onto her sister.

"Tea, I was sort of thinking beyond that…" Sea replied, sounding like she was picking her words with care. "I mean…how would you feel about getting away from Blight for a few weeks? If mum is better maybe the three of us could book a last-minute holiday? What do you think? Would you be able to take the time off work? I've got some leave to use up and it might help take your mind off Jack?"

"That would be great! The fruit farm is fairly casual, so that is fine, and I can always phone in sick at the library. My manager does it all the time. Thanks, Sea…"

"Hey, remember, there is no friend like a sister!" laughed Sea, although only for a second, before her tone became serious again, if not sombre.

"But, Tea, there is something else, something I thought about keeping to myself. You know me, I'm not really one to believe in the supernatural and premonitions and all that. But today, at the clinic…I don't know, I got a really bad feeling. Like mum was only ill, was only being kept where she was, because someone was making her sick. Deliberately, on purpose, without us really understanding how they did it. And that this meant bad things for you and me too? I don't know who would want to hurt us, or if I am thinking of murder or black magic, but I was suddenly convinced we were in real danger. All of us, as a family…."

"Sea! What are you saying???" Tea had never heard Elsie, her elder, sensible sister ever suggest something so off the wall before.

"Oh, just ignore me, Tea. I've probably been working too hard or not sleeping enough. Once we are on holiday, relaxing on the beach, you and mum can have a big laugh about how paranoid I've become. Never mind what I said, it'll be nice to get away for a while, right? Just picture yourself among the sand dunes…"

Chapter Eight: High Summer Fayre

Swept up in the heart of the procession, Tea fought to disentangle herself from the unruly ranks of people filing past, alert to any gap through which to escape. No matter how often she was exposed to it, this element of the High Summer Fayre never failed to disturb her. There was something grotesque about the sight of her fellow villagers prancing about in homemade costumes, the majority draped in garlands of flowers or sporting regalia fashioned from corn husks and briar, their faces concealed behind oversized animal masks. Meanwhile, out on the flanks, local musicians played endless variations on traditional jigs or beat a steady percussion on the drums that hung round their necks. Tea had never quite laid to rest the childhood fear that it was only on these occasions she was seeing her neighbours as they truly were; it was the rest of the time, when they appeared to be normal, that they were, in fact, in disguise.

Throughout a restless night and right up to the last minute, Tea had been adamant that she would not attend The Fayre. Yet by mid-morning the hours had begun to drag and Amber's invitation gradually grew more appealing. Anything to distract from those tormenting thoughts about Jack; the agonising guilt that overcame her whenever she was alone. Without being fully aware of her actions, by noon Tea was out the door and dressed for the village green, hoping that somehow she could lose herself in the summer crowds, with their brisk air of excitement and upraised voices drifting skywards like balloons. If nothing else The Fayre should, at least, fill the void until Sea appeared. On the front lawn she crossed paths with Mr Tender who, since shortly after dawn, she had seen steering wheelbarrows back and forth, piled high with earth. Tea supposed, in her mum's absence, it was really her responsibility to keep an eye on the gardener and approve any alterations he was making. Yet that hardly felt like a priority right now and, besides, when she glanced out the back windows, it all looked pretty enough. So instead of engaging Mr Tender in a business discussion she asked if he would be coming to the High Summer Fayre.

"Maybe later, Miss Felicity. There are a few things that need attending to first..."

The Fayre was already in full swing by the time Tea arrived. She felt as if she had been summoned from afar, lured across still, sweltering fields by the seductive call of sirens and megaphones. Although obviously intended as a celebratory affair, an annual display of Blight's community spirit, the occasion had always produced the opposite effect on Tea. Whilst her sister was off winning competitions or taking part in team sports, as a child she would wander off alone among the coconut shies and cake stalls, feeling like she had absolutely nothing in common with anybody else present. And, in her current state of mind, this year was hardly likely to be an improvement. Beneath the banners and bunting, the broad village green was bursting at the seams with historical enactments and fairground rides, the attractions spilling out into adjacent streets and shaded alleys. This left Tea faintly disorientated, blindly picking her way between the canvas tents that had sprung up like a city overnight. What exactly was she doing here, she wondered? Should she try and find Amber? Broadcast an announcement over the Tannoy system and ask to be collected, like a lost child?

Watching everybody swarming around her having a good time only increased her sense of alienation. Something about the High Summer Fayre had never sat right with Tea. There was too much emphasis on a shared identity, a collective memory. The adults drank their real ale and watched folk musicians perform, whilst their children were encouraged to take part in games and activities that promoted local history and affirmed the beliefs of their elders. Whether it was in her blood or in her head Tea did not know, yet her natural instinct was to be suspicious of, and resistant to, this gentle, underhand coercion. The entire spectacle reminded Tea of an uncomfortable evening she had spent as a young teenager, on one of those rare occasions she had been invited to stay over by a schoolmate; this rich girl who lived in a converted barn. The parents had come home drunk and insisted Tea and her friend turn their music off and listen to something 'more genuine, less commercial'. Tea had then looked on in horror as the couple had proceeded to folk-dance around their luxurious living room barefoot, earnestly exclaiming that they were 'gypsies at heart'.

With her mind elsewhere, Tea had inadvertently stumbled into the midst of one of the many processions weaving through the streets and circling the green, it's bizarre cast of characters presumably representing some tradition, the origins of which she, and hopefully everyone below a certain age, had quite forgotten. No doubt Ashton Veil would have approved of his village keeping such customs alive. But do traditions need to stay the same? Is it healthy to replay familiar scenes forever? Such ideas troubled Tea as she impatiently wrestled free from the clutches of The Hobby Horse and the unnerving, faceless figures of The Green Men, clad head to toe in leaves. Catching her breath, Tea again looked around for Amber. What location would she chose for staging this memorial service to Jack? Through the crowd, Tea spotted Mrs Stone presiding over one of the more extravagant stalls, furnished with a roped off seating area and serving strawberries and champagne to the village elite. However, she dared not interrupt Amber's mum mid-flow. Mrs Stone was clearly in her element, holding court over an elderly yet elegant clientele, only too keen to gratify their interest in the various items of china ferried to and fro by her select team of daintily dressed waitresses.

"The whole service has been kindly donated to us for the day by Harrow View House" Tea overheard her explaining, referring to a National Trust property situated on the border of Blight. "As you may know, I have long been one of their benefactors. If you look closely you can see a fine tracing of owls on each piece, the crest of the family who first…."

Tea smiled to herself as she recalled her own mother's many brave but disastrous attempts at contributing homemade cakes or pastries to the High Summer Fayre. 'Bake it…sieve it…knead it…' she would jovially announce to no-one in particular before once again making a mess of the kitchen table, her watching daughters well aware she had no idea what she was doing, later helping her to shovel the sugar and flour off the floor, as if it were snow. Mrs Stone and her kind belonged to another world and, content to leave them there, Tea pushed on through the fray, bypassing the maypole dancers and puppet shows, in search of people she recognised as friends of Jack. If only Karmilla were here, she thought sadly, all this would be so much more bearable then. Yes, all she needed was one close friend, or perhaps a few. Together they would see straight through all these outdated ceremonies and this fake bonhomie, exposing the darkness lurking beneath, the shadows that haunted the slides and carousels.

Overlooking one of the children's play areas, ringing with excited screams and hysterical tears, Tea did eventually run into someone she knew. A solitary, physically awkward figure loitered near the swings, as if awaiting his wife and child, although there was no sign of them in the immediate vicinity. As she approached, he turned to inspect her and, as always, let his eyes linger slightly too long.

"Hello, Felicity. That's an interesting outfit you're wearing…"

Great, frowned Tea, just my luck. Robin Dewar. On the positive side, considering his proclivities, he was bound to have taken note of Amber's movements. Tea asked her driving instructor if he knew where the vigil was being held.

"Why? Don't you know?"

This was one of Robin's endearing routines that Tea had been forced to endure over the last few months. An attempt at humour, or at least to amuse himself. Whenever she did not know the answer to a question or requested a piece of information, he would stare blankly at her for an extended period before replying, dispassionately 'Why? Don't you know?', savouring her frustration and discomfort. Tea did not have the patience for this today. As a matter of fact, if her driving lessons were over, she no longer had any reason to tolerate Robin's behaviour. Thus she made her excuses and moved on, roaming from the village green into the surrounding thoroughfares.

Away from the attractions, the mayhem of the music and rides, Tea was relieved to find the crowds thinning. In these clearings, Tea was granted more of an opportunity to survey the scene and seek out familiar faces. If Amber had any sense, she would surely have selected some secluded spot for Jack's service, sheltered from all the bustle and noise. As all the teenagers knew, Blight had plenty of back street meeting places and smaller green spaces, hidden away from the eyes of the public. Tea wondered how the others were coping today? Personally, she was already struggling with the contrast between the carnival atmosphere being conducted in front of her and the circus of despair she felt raging inside. Maybe Amber was right and coming together to mourn would help, giving everyone the confidence to open up a bit?

On the fringes of The Fayre the stalls had become less ambitious in scope and less professional in appearance, presided over by a motley array of local cranks and frustrated artists, hawking household bric-a-brac alongside their own creations, which consisted mainly of misshapen pottery and dreary water colour landscapes. As she navigated the labyrinth of cobbled lanes, Tea paid only the most superficial attention to these straggling stalls, that was until she was distracted by one display in particular. From the tickets placed next to the items that were arranged across the chequered tablecloth, it was clear this was intended as some kind of raffle, although nobody seemed to be putting much effort into promoting it. Stood to the side of the table, gossiping with another young couple who owned the adjacent plot, Tea noticed the local hairdressing team, Don and Michelle Grade. Apparently, karaoke was not their only side-line and they also shared a gift for village fetes.

"Hey there, can we help you?" purred Don as he slipped swiftly into position behind the table, moving like a well-oiled machine. Within seconds he was joined at the hip by his wife, known to always take an enthusiastic interest in whatever young woman her husband was talking to. Although she hardly ever got her hair cut by them, Tea was familiar with these two by reputation. Both tended to squeeze in a little too close when talking to you, as if they were constantly sizing you up for one of their supposed wife-swapping parties. The rumour around Blight was The Grades were having trouble recruiting babysitters these days. Word had got out they had a habit of returning early, sometimes together and sometimes alone, but always drunk and unannounced, as though hoping to take their sitter by surprise.

But today Tea was not concerned with the details of Don and Michelle's unsavoury 'open relationship'. They could carry on swinging for all she cared, swinging like a corpse in a noose. No, what had drawn her to their stall was a set of earrings labelled as a raffle prize. They looked identical to a rare pair of earrings that Karmilla often wore; in fact, Tea had been admiring them in the pub on their very last night together.

"Excuse me, where did you get these?"

"Oh…those…I'm really not sure…" faltered Michelle under the watchful eyes of her husband, no longer her typical, flirtatious self. "I think it was Mr Dodsworth, from 'The Restoration', who donated them. He said they had belonged to his niece. Right, Don?"

Tea delicately lifted the dangling earrings from the table. As she examined them, raising them up into the sunlight, they sparkled like they held a secret. Meanwhile, The Grades studied her in silence, maintaining their superficial smiles with perfect synchronicity, smiles that suggested they had something to hide. But they always look like that, Tea reminded herself, it does not necessarily mean they are mixed up in Karmilla's disappearance. Replacing the earrings, she thanked The Grades and walked away, whispering to herself under her breath: "I don't know…I don't know…" Perhaps it was all just a coincidence? Although the earrings had appeared unique to Tea, it was unlikely that Karmilla owned any designer jewellery. She had probably just snapped them up early from a high street store and in a few weeks the world would be full of people wearing them. Once again Tea cautioned herself against irrational, intrusive thoughts. She should have learnt to handle them by now. All she need do was to recognise them for what they were and then dismiss them without further debate. Whilst tackling this process, Tea completed a quick circuit of the centre of the village, without sighting Amber and friends. Of course the simple answer could be that her old classmates were still in bed and had not arrived yet. She was willing to bet they all went out last night anyway, despite what had happened to Jack; any excuse for a few drinks and some moments of melodrama.

At a loss for anything better to do, Tea made her way back towards the village green, this time approaching from a different angle. She would give them half an hour, no more. Any brief appeal the prospect of a wake had held was quickly waning. As happened too frequently, Tea felt like she had been talked into something against her better judgement. She would much rather mourn Jack alone, perhaps a private ceremony back at home, locked away with only the cat for company. Or, alternatively, she could wait until this evening and unload her emotions on Sea. Frankly, either option was preferable to attempting to share her feelings with Jack's idiotic, over privileged friends. More than likely, their minds had already moved on to their upcoming gap years, exploring exotic beaches with all expenses paid. This might involve a bit of charity work on behalf of the impoverished locals on the side but, more importantly, they would be provided with plenty of fuel for dinner party chatter over the years to come.

Pitched on the corner of the green closest to Tea was an unusually elaborate tent, every inch of canvas decorated with what looked like images from a Victorian fairy painting; a clutter of waxing moons, darting sprites and cute animals that appeared endearing on first sight, but grew slightly disconcerting the more attention you gave. Judging from the excited queue of little girls gathered outside, and the endless stream shimmering and fluttering past as they exited, Tea guessed this must be a Fairy Tent. Even as a child, she had never felt at ease in such places, watching on like a wallflower as little princesses were adorned with glitter makeup and gossamer wings. However, she did have a vague memory of her sister one summer, enthusiastically waving a wand around whilst wearing a tinfoil tiara. At the front of a queue, as always, was a young girl that Tea recognised as Amber's little sister, Coral. The baby of the family, spoiled rotten and supremely confident for her age, Coral was waiting in line, impatiently, beside her father. Mr Stone was something important in real estate with, it was rumoured, a stake in Harrow View House. Yet he was also a shadowy figure, rarely seen, hence the widely held belief that he owed his success to the influence of his wife. Hoping Amber's sister would remember her from the fleeting occasions they had met, Tea went across to ask if she knew where today's vigil was taking place. Coral shook her head with a petulant pout and took a step closer to her father, as if she feared the commoners were getting too close, overstepping the mark. Mr Stone and his daughter were then ushered inside the tent without offering Tea any further acknowledgement.

Now fully prepared to head home, Tea was about to turn away from The Fairy Tent when she caught a glimpse of the interior which was, as might be expected, illuminated only by fairy lights. The décor had been designed to resemble a dusky woodland grove and through the artificial twilight, beyond the hazy visions of children flitting about draped in twinkling gauze, Tea had seen Mr Tender's nephew Elvin, sat cross-legged at the back on one of the fake tree stumps. Seemingly restored to full health, he was observing proceedings with a condescending sneer, watching as a team of middle-aged women attached wings and handed out wands to their young charges, whilst the parents stood around making small talk and looking bored. Curiosity was drawing Tea back towards the tent. She wondered if the lady apparently overseeing proceedings could be Elvin's mother; the tragic, enigmatic sister that Mr Tender had made such an object of mystery? In-between applying makeup to smiling faces and stitching on stars, this pale, willowy figure frequently glanced over to where Elvin sat and requested, affectionately, that he fetch things on her behalf. Tea noticed that, even when laughing, there was a certain haunted look that never quite left the lady's eyes, betraying her attempts at frivolity. With the restless queue already in disarray, Tea had no problems slipping inside unnoticed. She had been seized by a sudden, unshakeable conviction that she must speak to Mr Tender's sister at all costs, if this was indeed her. However, Elvin must have registered Tea's entrance immediately, as she had only advanced a few steps before he intercepted her, the self-satisfied smile replaced by a scowl.

"This is the one!" he hissed, loud enough to turn heads.

"Oh…hello Elvin…I just wanted to…I just wanted to know if you were feeling any better?" floundered Tea, aware that all eyes were now upon her, including the desolate, dejected gaze of the woman in charge of The Fairy Tent.

"This is her! The girl from The Veil House!"

As he spat out these words, Elvin's body appeared to Tea to twist, almost coil, in the semi-darkness. His entire frame grew taut and he started to tremble, as though he were about to succumb to another of his seizures.

"No, Elvin, it's me…don't you remember? Felicity Greene. From 'The Burrows'…"

"It's the girl from The Veil House! It's the girl from The Veil House!" he violently insisted, resolute in his belief as to Tea's identity.

Alarmed, intimidated, she began to retreat. Although everybody else present was blatantly as bewildered by Elvin's behaviour as she was, nobody made any effort to intervene. That was until the lady that Tea took for Elvin's mother, looking more otherworldly than ever, floated through the crowd towards her. They regarded each for a second, perplexed, as if neither were sure if they were dreaming the other.

"Who are you?" The woman asked Tea in an ethereal voice. "Where do you come from?"

"I'm not sure…" murmured Tea, wishing she were anywhere else. "I can't remember…"

The woman reached out a hand to touch her cheek, perhaps needing to confirm whether this girl who stood before her was a ghost. But Tea drew back, then turned and fled the tent. She pushed her way through the hordes circling The Fayre in the sunshine, her whole being urging her to get as far away from the village green as possible. What had Elvin been going on about? Why was he so obsessed with this idea that she lived at The Veil House? Tea had no time to gather her thoughts before she sighted Amber's mob approaching, a motley dozen looking tired but in perfect harmony, implying that they had all slept over at the same place.

"Tea! You're not leaving? We were hoping you would join us for Jack's thing? Everyone wants you there..." Despite Amber's emphatic assurance, the rest of her rabble looked completely indifferent as to whether Tea was present or not.

"I'm sorry, Amber, I can't stay..." blurted Tea, a tinge of social anxiety coming to the fore. "My sister is picking me up this evening. I'm going away with Elsie for a while..."

"You're leaving the village???" Amber looked utterly astounded, as if the suggestion that someone wanted to leave Blight, or indeed was able to, was the most implausible, preposterous thing she had ever heard. Yet, just as quickly, she recovered herself. "When? What time tonight?"

"That depends on a few things. Probably not until late, but I need to get ready...." Tea knew that Amber could tell she was brushing her off but, in truth, she no longer cared. "Sorry to bail out, I just need some space..."

Amber and friends were obviously unimpressed, angered at being snubbed by someone who should not be in a position to do so. Tea understood that by shunning the vigil she probably came across as heartless. But she knew all too well the depth of her feelings and, besides, she suspected the others were only playacting, treating Jack's death as if it were a party game, an excuse for seeking attention. Walking away, Tea could feel Amber giving her the evil eye behind her back, quietly reigning down curses on her head. Her crime? She stood accused of deserting her duties, breaking ranks with the peer group she should be seeking to court. For Tea, this felt like a defining moment; there was no turning back now.

****

On departing the village green, Tea pretended to herself she did not know where she was going, that she had no destination in mind but home. Yet, try as she might to shut her eyes to the trajectory her feet were taking, it eventually became impossible to ignore that she was bound for The Veil House. Why else would she be leaving the lane at this precise point, scrambling up the verge to hike the trail that weaved through the woods, high above her neighbour's houses? Tea justified her curiosity as inevitable after what had happened in The Fairy Tent. Yet part of her knew this had simply provided her with the excuse to return, an opportunity that, in secret, she had been patiently awaiting. Here, as she passed, were the now familiar landmarks of HarmWood: the drab, lifeless pools that nobody ever visited, the crumbling ruins of walls that led nowhere and, lost amid the undergrowth, the stone monument with the strange writing. But it was by sound as well as sight that Tea knew her path; the ever-present whispering in the wilderness, full of half-heard promises and broken charms, enticing her onwards. The trees appeared to stand aside, ushering The Veil House into view, a raised temple to a realm of shadows, steeped in shame even on a summer's afternoon. Tea took a tentative step closer, a little afraid of entering its sphere, of falling under a malign influence. Why had she come here? What was she looking for behind those blank windows, in those dusty rooms she could only picture clearly in her dreams? Was this merely another of her misguided infatuations? Brooding alone, The Veil House offered no answers, arched against a tiered backdrop of trees and greenery that simmered beyond the heat haze. Tea felt suddenly drowsy, as though she had been drugged. Why didn't she just lie down here, curl up on the grass and languish at The Veil House forever?

Summoning a strength she did not know she possessed, Tea shook herself free of the spell and turned away. 'Pull yourself together, Felicity!' What was she playing at? She was wasting time dwelling on the past when she should be at home right now, preparing for the future. What time was it anyway? Sea would be annoyed if she were not packed and ready to go. At that instant her phone sprang into life, the shrill ringtone disrupting the pensive silence of the surrounding woodland. Tea fumbled in her bag, taken by surprise; there was usually no signal this far out.

"Hi…Tea…can you hear me? I'm at the clinic…" It was her sister, right on cue.

"You're a bit faint, but I can hear you. How is mum? Have you spoken to her?"

"Not yet…in the car park…about to go in…" Reception was fading in and out, broken up by the trees, who appeared to frown on such a coarse intrusion. "But everything is arranged at the hospital…a bed ready…just need Chalk to sign…"

"Hello? Sea? Are you still there? I lost you for a minute…"

"Hang on…" the muffled sounds of movement, a car door opening and closing. "Any better? Just to warn you…I'm running a bit late. But I'll definitely be there some time this evening. And don't worry, my next-door neighbour has agreed to look after Whispers. Oh…one last thing before I go…"

The line began to crackle and drone again, casting Sea adrift in a squall that made her sound like she was slowly sinking beneath the waves. Tea had to concentrate to hear her sister above the static until, abruptly, clarity was rekindled in a rush of words, as if Sea were gasping for air:

"I forgot to say. When I was last at the clinic and looking in those little rooms, guess who I saw? Guess who one of the patients was?"

"Oh Sea, I really have no idea. Surprise me…"

"It was that gardener that mum knows. What was his name? The one she always meant to hire. Mr Tender!"

Following a series of electronic stutters and distorted, isolated words, this time their conversation was terminated for good. Tea stood shell shocked in the clearing, clutching her phone and frantically attempting to text her sister or return the call. But HarmWood had pulled ranks and was having none of it; the connection was severed.

The full impact of Sea's news took a while to register but, gradually, Tea began to turn it over. If her sister was to be believed, if she had indeed seen the real Mr Tender in hospital…

…then who was that man at home, practically living in her back garden?

Chapter Nine: The Candlelit Letter

'The gardener is not really the gardener…the gardener is not really the gardener…'

The one phrase kept running through Tea's head like a broken record, taunting her as she strove to grasp its implications. OK, assuming her sister was right and Mr Tender truly was an impostor, then this changed everything. Tea need no longer think ill of herself, for here at last was tangible evidence that a threat existed. And in the real world, not just her imagination. But what possible motive could there be for posing as a friend of her mother's? A flurry of erratic, improbable conspiracy theories rushed forward to present themselves. Could this be the corroboration she had been seeking? Was there indeed some diabolic plot against her family, in which the whole village was implicated? Perhaps, as Sea had proposed, foul play was responsible for putting both her mum and the real Albert Tender in hospital. The more Tea thought about it, the more indisputable it seemed; the proof had been right before her eyes if only she had known how to look. Yes, there was intrigue involving everyone, the locals were in league against Tea and her mum, keeping them prisoners within the confines of Blight whilst simultaneously exiling them to the perimeters. Tea could not prevent a wry smile from forming on her lips. After all this time fearing the worst, the final revelation almost came as a relief. Better late than never.

With the menace exposed and the prime suspect identified, the initial, paralysing wave of fear soon dissipated in the late afternoon sun. Tea felt validated, fuelled by a revitalized faith in her own point of view, her ability to see through smokescreens. I know what this is, she thought, this is one of those pivotal moments I've read about, if it is possible to recognise such a thing when it occurs. But what should be her first move? Regardless of her newfound confidence she dared not confront Mr Tender, or the man masquerading as him, quite yet. This meant she would need to avoid returning to 'The Burrows', at least until nightfall, by which time she hoped the gardener would have kept his word and joined the festivities at the High Summer Fayre. So, how to spend the hours in-between? Without a friend to confide in, with no one else to turn to, Tea wheeled around to face The Veil House once more. The upper windows held her stare until she was forced to look away, overcome by their mournful aspect. Nevertheless, Tea observed that the front door, as ever, hung loose on its hinges, an open invitation to any who had lost their way. The encroaching woodland seemed to beckon you to shelter beneath the roof. Hadn't Elvin said that this was her house? Her ancestral home? Then what more productive way to waste a few hours than by inspecting her property and drawing up an inventory? Who knows, perhaps she would even unearth some priceless family heirloom, something of value?

'The key is in the roots…'

Determined to probe deeper into the secrets of The Veil House than she ever had before, Tea strode back towards the crooked edifice, flinching only slightly when she fell under its shadow. Squeezing through the gap in the door, she was immediately struck by the contrast in temperature, the constant chill within compared to the woozy heat without. Emphasising the arctic atmosphere, fittings and fixtures appeared to have been frozen in time, rooms unchanged since the vague memories of her last, fleeting visit. Tea and a couple of classmates had crept inside and ran a circuit of the front room before rushing out again. It had been that endmost summer, the last one before everyone had decided they were too old for such childish games. And to this day the property still lay largely empty, the odd chair or sideboard sitting at an awkward angle in the middle of the floorboards, smothered in dust. Some must have returned as teenagers, for scattered about her feet were empty beer bottles and discarded cigarette butts, yet the litter was so minimal as to suggest nobody had stayed for long. Tea made a quick survey of the downstairs rooms, ducking under low ceilings sagging with damp, disturbing rats and spiders that scuttled from her path. However, she decided against attempting the staircase to the second floor. The bannisters hung limp like broken arms and every other step was splintered; an unreliable, genuinely dangerous assault course. There was no point in another family member ending up in hospital. In the half light, Tea instead made her way towards the back of the house, steered by the sporadic streams of sunlight that seeped through holes punctured high up in the walls. Gritting her teeth, she wrenched open one final, resistant door, which squealed as if being dragged from a profound sleep.

Tea found herself in the ruined conservatory she had seen from the rear of the property, the room ruptured by a tree that had perhaps once been a pruned, decorative novelty but was now dislodging roof tiles as it fanned out, dominating the living space. Actually, from this perspective, the room resembled a nursery more than a conservatory, with a cot abandoned in one corner and, peeling from the walls, what looked like the remnants of faded, fairy-tale wallpaper. Tea glanced around sadly at the artefacts of someone's lost childhood.

'The key is in the roots...'

Amidst the silence of The Veil House, Tea felt as though an imp were whispering in her ear, reminding her of the riddle she had uncovered in her mum's room, that puzzling message scrawled on the back of a photograph. Although Tea had continued to ponder this mystery in spare moments, with all that had been going on it was one of many things she had pushed to the back of her mind. Yet now the desire to resolve the matter returned, this time with an increased urgency. Well, all trees have roots, she reasoned, so this would be as good a place as any to start searching. After all, perhaps it was fate that Elvin had directed her here, whether he had acted intentionally or not. He was such an odd character, an outsider as much as she was, that Tea could not determine his motives. Perhaps he sympathised and wanted to help? Had Elvin, the boy with the spriteful, glittering green eyes and air of detachment in some way sensed that the leads she needed lay hidden at The Veil House? If so, then this was not the only link. For there was the photograph itself, depicting her mum with an unidentified male companion, posing before a house that looked very much like this one, before the rot set in. As the dust motes hung suspended, Tea talked herself into it. This must be the place.

But what exactly was she looking for? From that cursory note provided with the photograph, Tea could not even tell if 'key' was meant literally or was intended as a metaphor. Uncertain where to begin, she knelt down to examine the foot of the trunk in the hope of tracing an inscription carved in the bark or locating a treasure map stashed in a hollow; anything to give her a head start. But luck was not on her side this evening, leaving her with only the most rudimentary option. Tea began digging in the earth that had been exposed beneath the uprooted floor tiles, clawing and shovelling the dirt aside with her bare hands. As she worked the daylight began to fade which was, surprisingly, a source of comfort. Tea would die of embarrassment if she were witnessed employed in such a senseless, demented task. What if some belated rambler, descending the slopes, happened to peer into the interior of the gutted house? At least, at this hour, she melted into nothingness; just another shadow. Her hunched silhouette also extended across the conservatory, throwing shapes upon the wall that reminded Tea of the games she had once played with her sister, sculpting their hands in front of the bedside lamp to create a shadow theatre of witches, fairies and fluttering birds.

****

Having dredged up nothing of significance, in what already seemed like hours, Tea's enthusiasm for her mission began to wane. Not only were her hands and clothes soiled with mud but also, not for the first time in recent months, she had started to question her sanity. In the mottled gloom behind broken bay windows it felt like four in the morning, a time Tea had heard was when madness reached its peak. Yet, outside, a rosy dusk was settling on the summer's evening, promising fond memories for all. So why was she shut up indoors, toiling away at tree roots in the distant hope of understanding her past? Worms, fossils and the occasional shard of shattered pottery passed through her fingers, but no key to her family history. Tea sank back on her haunches, on the point of giving up the ghost.

"Bake it, sieve it, knead it. The past is only what you feed it…" she muttered forlornly to herself.

As if by magic, in the dying embers of the day, a declining ray of sunlight streaked across the floorboards, catching an object that glinted like silver among a mound of earth she had excavated earlier. Worried that the spell would fade, that she would soon be unable to detect the source in the gathering darkness, Tea shunted over into the path of the beam. Leaning in close, she carefully sifted the debris to extract the article from its grave, wiping away the clinging twigs and clumps of moss. Lying in her palm was a small key! Tea blinked her eyes…once…twice. Yes, it was still there. Almost unbelievable but undoubtedly a real key, not an image from a dream or a figure of speech. And her intuition told her it would be the perfect fit for the tin box she had discovered beneath her mum's wardrobe. As the light in the room dwindled again, Tea bathed in her reward. So, after all that time spent speculating and agonising, the answer really was that simple! Eager to get home and test the lock, she pocketed the key and hurriedly collected her things, feeling like she had outstayed her welcome. It was odd; as she exited the front door she had a sudden sense of déjà vu, as though she had left The Veil House under similar, pressing circumstances once before, but too far in the past to remember clearly. Dismissing the notion, Tea struck out from beneath the eaves, entering the woods.

Night was descending much too quickly as she marched along, summoning up a new set of fears. After dark, without the Dutch courage supplied by a night of drinking, Tea was worried she might lose her way along the route home. What if, without the subtle yet reliable milestones of daylight hours, she was doomed to spend the entire night walking in circles? Already Tea was finding it difficult to see that far ahead, the darkness merging the woodland scenery into an indistinguishable mass of barbed outlines. Every direction looked the same and every track appeared to narrow with the night. To sustain momentum, Tea was forced to grapple aside the grasping, quivering branches that grazed her skin and tore at her hair. 'They want to blind me', she almost persuaded herself, 'they want to poke out my eyes so I

123

can never find my way home!' Yet shielding her face she ploughed on, ignoring the repeated scratches and irregular undulations of the ground that caused her to stagger like she was drunk. Inevitably, before long Tea hit a dead end, confronted with an impenetrable wall of briar, blocking her path. She had never encountered this barrier on previous walks home which meant, unless some enchantment had caused it to spring up overnight, she must have taken a wrong turn.

Recounting her steps to what passed for a crossroads (a clearing where several worn bridleways intersected), Tea attempted to recover her bearings. As she scrutinised the immediate vicinity, a shiver ran down her spine. She was conscious of a silent, unseen presence, watching her intently from a short distance. Perhaps acknowledging detection, a shade slipped fluidly from the foliage, advancing low to the ground. A pair of incandescent eyes made visible; swirling, golden orbs piercing the darkness.

"Noosha!"

The fox paused a few feet from Tea, appearing to wait expectantly for her to follow. She accepted the invitation without a second thought, confident that Noosha, unlike so many of her acquaintances, only possessed the best of intentions. Initially the pair maintained a brisk pace through the benighted woodland, Tea following in the wake of the fox as they negotiated a maze of unmarked trails, hidden to the human eye. However, the closer they got to 'The Burrows' the more cautious Noosha seemed to become, slowing to a trot and frequently stopping to scent the air in suspicion. Put on guard by the animal's behaviour, Tea strained to hear the warning signs that had so evidently alarmed her guide. When she held her breath it felt as though the trees did too, allowing previously subdued sounds to rise to the surface. Somewhere, not too far off, the snapping of twigs and crackle of dead leaves. It was possible this was simply the customary patter and rustle of wildlife, foraging in the scrub. On the other hand, it could mean that there were others abroad in HarmWood, besides herself. Only, it made no sense for anyone else to be out here at this hour. There were no houses in the vicinity aside from her own and not one of these paths provided a short cut anywhere. Also, if someone were holding an impromptu, post-Fayre party, surely the traffic would be more obvious? Tea was fast running out of explanations. Perhaps she was being stalked through the woods by the ghostly footsteps of 'The Lady Outside'? Whatever the answer, she was prepared to take a risk and felt a growing impatience with Noosha's reticence. The key she had found was burning a hole in her pocket; awaiting her at home was a trove of secrets.

Daydreaming, Tea was taken by surprise when the fox abruptly doubled back and veered from the path they had been travelling, scampering away through the ferns in what was surely the opposite direction to her house. Still, she felt she had no choice but to trust in Noosha's enhanced night vision and followed obediently. Although continuing to remain alert, by now Tea had to accept she was completely lost, cutting a convoluted route through woodland scenery that might as well have been native to another planet. And yet, eventually, like a distant moon drawing closer, she caught a glimpse of her own twilit garden, albeit approached at a different angle from usual. Tea breathed a sigh of relief. In stoic silence, Noosha had successfully plotted a course that skirted the strange manoeuvres underway in HarmWood, safely depositing her at her back door. Perhaps it was the man who pretended to be Mr Tender they had heard walking so late in the woods, for he no longer appeared to be on the premises. At least if he has gone home that is one hurdle cleared, thought Tea, relaxing a little. With that she turned to pet Noosha, to thank her for escorting her home, only to find the fox had already vanished, reclaimed by the darkness from whence she came.

Hesitating on the edge of HarmWood, Tea reflected how in days past the back garden before her had felt like home, a safe place to spend time and let down her guard. Yet lately, she had never felt quite at ease there. Where once the garden had been sprawling and unkempt in a comforting way, warm and familiar like a baggy jumper or an unmade bed, now the atmosphere was one of cold-hearted hostility and disorder. It had seemed that way ever since the afternoon she lost her way and witnessed Elvin's collapse. No, before that. Ever since…?

Ever since the new gardener had first arrived. Tea realised she might be catastrophizing but, until she understood why he had deceived her, the thought that this 'Mr Tender' had infiltrated her home terrain was distressing enough. Hence tonight she hurtled down the garden path as if chased by The Hound of the Baskervilles. Letting herself in to the kitchen, Tea made certain that, this evening, she remembered to lock the door behind her. She was promptly greeted by the plaintive cries of a cat, yet not for once around her feet, but from some point that sounded incredibly remote, a muted echo from a million miles away. Tea groaned in frustration; she really did not have time for this tonight. Was Whispers lost again? Shut in somewhere? Although she went through the motions of searching the house, ascending and descending the stairs, banging on doors and opening cupboards, her heart was not really in it and she failed to find the cat. Throughout her search Tea caught Whispers intermittent bouts of whining and yet, curiously, no matter where she was the sounds never seemed to be getting any closer. It was almost as if the cat's cries were rising from somewhere underneath the house, yet 'The Burrows' boasted no cellar or crawlspace.

"Wait for me, Whispers…" pleaded Tea as she climbed back up the stairs to her mum's room. "Don't worry, I won't leave you behind…" But before she could summon the courage to consider the future, she first needed some answers concerning her past.

There had never been any doubt in Tea's mind that the key she had found would unlock the box beneath the wardrobe. Even as far afield as The Veil House, submerged in shadow, she had known where it belonged as soon as she had seen it blink. So, being aware that this grand opening might prove to be a significant moment in her life, Tea chose to leave all the upstairs lights off, carrying only a flickering candle into her mum's bedroom, wanting to give the occasion an air of ceremony. Carefully removing the tin box from its resting place, as though she were retrieving a sacred pearl from the ocean floor, Tea peeled the photograph off the underside and placed both objects side by side on the carpet. Kneeling over the photo in the ill-lit room, she studied the image again. The harder Tea looked, the more convinced

126

she was that not only was her mum stood on the back lawn of The Veil House but that the baby in her arms was herself, not Sea. Next, sitting there in unassuming silence, was the tin box, its secrets sealed within, like a little tomb. Hands shaking, Tea slid the key into the lock and turned it. With a sharp click the lid sprung open, leading you to expect a musical box with a ballerina pirouetting awkwardly to an ancient tune. There was music, a brief refrain from a song long set aside, but this played only in Tea's head. The sole content of the box was, in fact, a few sheets of lined paper, neatly folded and apparently torn from your average notepad. From the few lines visible on the final page, Tea recognised her mum's handwriting, as seen on various shopping lists and post-its taped to the fridge. "It's a letter!" she gasped out loud. How romantic and old fashioned, smiled Tea; a letter somehow felt so much more private and intimate than a text or e-mail, suggesting time devoted and details that required attention, like when someone loaned you their favourite book. She gathered the pages up into her lap and began to read by candlelight:

Dearest Tea….

Discovering that the letter was actually addressed to her, and intended for her eyes alone, did to some degree assuage the twinge of guilt Tea had felt on opening the box, whilst also immediately increasing her anxiety. Yet she swallowed hard and forced herself to dive, fearlessly, into the body of the letter, braced for the impact of whatever she may encounter.

Dearest Tea,

If you are reading this then what I was most afraid of has come true and I am no longer there with you. I can only start by saying I'm sorry. There were so many times over the years I wanted to tell you what I am about to tell you now. Yet I convinced myself that if I kept quiet our problems might somehow fade away and speaking out loud would only bring back a past that was best forgotten. There were even moments I persuaded myself there was no need to explain as you must already know everything I wanted to tell you. It was just the way you looked at me sometimes, or certain things you said. So please forgive me if it seems I took the coward's way out but it has always been easier for me to write things down. And besides I knew that in the end your gifts would find you whether I spelled things out or not.

Do you understand what I mean by your 'gifts'? I know that like me you tend to hide a lot of what you are feeling from the world. So it is difficult even for a mother to see what is inside you. But there were signs from an early age that you were different from your sister. I can't really put these differences into words and before I go any further I want you to understand that this is not a bad thing. What I am about to tell you should not affect your relationship with Sea in any way. It always makes me proud to see what a strong bond you have with your sister. In my line of work you soon learn this does not happen in every family. So what you read next should not change how you feel about each other. The 'gifts' I am talking about may owe a little to me, but you have inherited more from your father's side. Which is why I addressed this letter to you rather than your sister.

Gary Greene is not your biological father. I can't write it any other way. If you are angry at me for not telling you earlier all I can say in my defence is there always felt like good reasons for this at the time. I never meant to trick you or lie to you. I suppose I told myself the truth was not important and perhaps it need not be. You were too young to really remember Gary and the short time you spent together. But believe me he was the one who acted like a true father to you. Gary protected us and cared for you the best he could, seeing as how young we all were back then. Which is more than can be said for your 'other father'. I've spent years being careful never to mention his name in front of you, hiding the evidence that he ever existed. In the back of my mind I was always afraid you might learn the truth from school bullies or local gossip. But fortunately for me the subject still seems to be taboo around Blight, even after all this time. Your biological father was a man named Ashton Veil. He lived not far from 'The Burrows' at a place people used to know as Blackwood Manor. Nowadays the kids call it 'The Veil House'. And for the first two years of your life we lived there too.

Before your mind starts racing, I'm afraid there is no point in looking for your father. Ashton Veil is long gone from Blackwood Manor and I believe him to be dead. Please do not take this as the loss it might feel at first. As I discovered too late Ashton Veil never cared for us and his interest in you was not born out of fatherly affection. Ask your sister if you want a second opinion but I doubt she will have been old enough to understand what was happening. Her memories are probably confused by all that being ferried back and forth between houses and families. Besides, I think Sea tends to dwell less on the past than you do. It is more her nature to forget and move forward. My only excuse for my behaviour is that Gary and I married very young. When I gave birth to Sea I was still only a teenager. With hindsight when I first met Veil I was at a crossroads in my life. On one hand I was happy and secure and raising a family but on the other a part of me still longed for adventure and feared my life was already over before it had really begun. Basically, back then I was nothing but a wide-eyed, rose-tinted girl...

Tea had tried not to permit herself any pauses, set on ploughing through the letter from beginning to end, without hesitations or time-outs to absorb the shock. Yet from the first sentence she began to feel her body tingling all over, as if she had been struck by a magic wand or her soul had been summoned from her body to float above, looking down. Tea gripped the sheaf of papers tighter in an attempt to stop her thoughts straying from the page, but it was increasingly difficult to concentrate with her mind inventing stories of its own, imaginings that escaped the margins. Her mum was in the middle of accounting for her actions, detailing how she had been preyed upon by the older, more experienced Veil, groomed into his way of thinking.

At first he seemed so exciting and exotic, like a reminder of something I had lost. You see, like me, he came from another place...

Tea felt she could certainly relate to that constant, underlying feeling of being an outcast, now more than ever. However, as to Veil's true history, whether he was local to Blight or had studied abroad and travelled widely, it sounded like her mum had got no closer to the truth than she had. Nevertheless, she had clearly fallen under the man's spell and followed her heart, throwing caution to the wind.

I'm not proud that I left Gary but that is what I did. And for a while I was sure I was happy, especially when I found I was pregnant with you. That summer it felt as if everything had fallen into place. That I had taken a risk but made the right choice. Finally I could see my future unfolding in front of me...

During this honeymoon period, the impression was that Veil had made a concentrated effort to charm Tea's mum with his philosophies. Apparently he liked to bombard her with lectures about freedom and liberty, promising her that he had rediscovered some basic truths about man and nature that would enable them to 'take back control' of the their lives. Being a bit of a dreamer, Tea could appreciate how her mum might have been attracted to this idea of her and Veil as outlaws, the only people capable of seeing through the petty rules and misinformation that society inflicted upon them. Especially when, as the letter laid out, Veil was beginning to gather quite a crowd around him; eminent locals who were enthused by his ideas and wanted to belong. What began quietly, inconsequentially, with discreet discussions at community functions and invitations to dinner had soon progressed to larger gatherings attended by up to a dozen guests. Whilst admitting to feeling a touch 'starstruck' at suddenly finding herself at the centre of local high society, Tea's mum confessed that, privately, she had begun to develop misgivings about both Veil's motives and his beliefs. Increasingly, she had the feeling that the group were concealing their true intentions from her, that visitors to Blackwood Manor would fall quiet whenever she stumbled across their hushed conversations on the lawn.

I can't pinpoint exactly when I first noticed something was wrong. There probably wasn't a particular day or a specific incident. It was more a feeling of unease that built up over time and deepened when I joined the dots. But not being native to Blight, with no family ties to the area, it was easy for Veil to isolate me and make me doubt myself. I realise that now. And the more confident he was that I had grown dependent on him, the more controlling his behaviour became. Yet even at my most alone he didn't quite have the hold over me that he thought. Although I never said a word I started to see the flaws in his opinions and to pick holes in everything he was encouraging me to accept. All this talk of a return to the 'The Old Ways' no longer sounded romantic to me. If anything it seemed the opposite, reactionary and cruel. But the hardest thing for me was that I appeared to be the only person around Veil thinking this. And sometimes I was scared he could read my mind...

Tea realised she was being dragged in and tore herself away from the letter again. She was severely tempted to simply hold the pages over

130

the naked flame and watch as her mother's words were reduced to cinders. Why should she listen to this plea for understanding after being lied to all these years? Tea felt her muscles tense, her insides knotting with a rage more acute than the result of one of her typical triggers, the candle before her fluttering erratically and sending shadows dancing around the bedroom walls. And yet, in spite of herself, she did feel some sympathy for her mum, identifying with the loneliness of her predicament. She must have struggled in silence as the sole heretic in a devoted congregation; wrestled with her conscience as she peeled away Veil's tolerant, easy going veneer to discover that, underneath it all, her partner felt absolute contempt for anyone who did not share his tastes, his priorities and his privilege. With nowhere else to run her mum had even, in secret, started visiting 'The Burrows' again, guilty but glad of any comfort that Gary could offer her. Unfortunately, that window had closed when he suddenly fell ill, struck down by a wasting sickness that Dr Chalk could not identify but implied might be highly contagious.

Gradually I found myself left out of group discussions and reduced to eavesdropping on Veil's telephone conversations to piece together what he and his followers had in mind. From what I could gather they were preparing for some prestigious event which was set to take place in HarmWood on the night of the High Summer Fayre. And yet when Veil and I were alone things were different, or at least for a while I believed they were. As much as he was able he continued to be warm and attentive. Only the more so after you were born. This calmed my fears to a point or perhaps just allowed me to turn a blind eye to some unpleasant truths. Looking back I suppose that is why I stayed in the relationship longer than I should have. Stupid as it may sound I hoped that if I wished hard enough and ignored all the warning signs this façade of a happy family life would somehow become a reality. Anyway, I didn't go with Veil to The High Summer Fayre that year, even though he had helped organise it. I don't know why. Probably I was afraid of bumping into members of Gary's family. So that evening you and I were by ourselves at Blackwood Manor. It was dusk when I left you in your cot in the conservatory and went for a quick stroll around the back garden, hoping to clear my head. Trust me Tea I was only outside a few minutes but they must have been watching us, waiting for the opportunity. When I got back you were gone!

Tea continued to read but with a sick, giddy feeling slowly rising from her stomach. The next paragraph seemed to suggest that either she was the victim of some elaborate prank or that her mother had always, secretly, been completely mad. And this madness would, of course, be hereditary, which must be why Tea found it so hard to discount what followed. On the surface, her mum appeared to be spinning some old folktale about her baby being kidnapped from her cot and spirited away to the forest. But, taking into account recent revelations, the accumulation of her suspicions and research, Tea could not bring herself to dismiss what she read so easily. Once she had come to terms with the initial shock, her mum claimed she instinctively knew that Veil's associates had stolen her child (*"Perhaps it was some kind of sixth sense, an ability I may have passed on to you"*). Although she could not yet grasp their purpose, she was sure it must have something to do with what she had overheard of the 'secret event', scheduled to take place that night, following The High Summer Fayre. Tea's mum recalled running in a blind frenzy through dark woods. Yet she was drawn towards the murmur of voices, a low chanting that rose and fell *"like prayers in church, only these words sounded strange and strangled as if spoken backwards"*. Accompanying this chorus was a frail, flickering light that illuminated the trees up ahead; a fire in the heart of HarmWood. Creeping in closer, she observed a circle of shrouded figures gathered around the flames, conducting some strange ceremony in a secluded glade. Naturally Veil was leading the proceedings, perched upon a pile of rocks that he used like a lectern.

There is not space here to explain exactly what Veil's sect hoped to achieve. If you want to find out more, if it is essential that you do so, you must somehow get access to that locked room in the library where you work. That is where they have stored their books ever since removing them from Blackwood Manor. 'Grimoires' they call them. All you need to know is that it was Veil's belief that he carried a rare blood type that placed him in a direct line of descent from ancient beings he referred to as 'The Old Ones'. You may think this sounds crazy but I beg you to trust me in spite of all you have just read. His ambition was to summon these entities back from history and restore a sacred past that he and his followers called 'The Old Ways'. Yet a special ritual was required to accomplish this. A ritual which involved a spilling of this rare blood. Of course Veil was too cowardly to offer himself as a sacrifice so he used me to deliver him an heir. Yes, Tea, you were to be the chosen victim. All at once, but far too late, everything I had imagined suddenly made sense. For an instant, I was too stunned to act. But when Veil raised your tiny form up to the night sky, when I heard you cry out in fright, something must have snapped deep inside of me...

Whatever mistakes she had made in the early days, and overlooking all the confrontations that had occurred since, Tea felt tears well in her eyes when she learnt how much her mum had sacrificed. According to the letter, she had thrown herself recklessly towards the fire, breaking the circle and scattering the participants. Wrestling her baby from the arms of Veil, she fled the scene and the pandemonium that erupted in her wake, her only concern to get as far away from that terrible place as possible. Clearly the coven had not been prepared for such an intrusion, such an unexpected disruption in the order of things. Escaping into the woods, Tea's mother had been forced to avoid various cult members who were behaving like lost sheep, running aimlessly in rings and bleating in fear. Then, she heard another sound, carrying from a distance:

I suppose it must have been Veil who let out the inhuman, ear piercing scream. Who knows? I'm not sure I even care. I certainly didn't go back and check.

Afterwards, the rumour circulated that, starved of Tea's blood, 'The Old Ones' had instead taken her father as their sacrifice, dragging Veil off at speed through the treetops. If this is honestly what happened, Tea supposed there may have been a kernel of truth in what he preached, the abilities he claimed to possess, even though his methods and ideals were all wrong. Gary, meanwhile, had been charitable enough to allow her mother to move back into 'The Burrows', reuniting Tea with her sister. The letter depicted the ensuing years as the calm after the storm however, reading between the lines, Tea wondered if her mum was deliberately deluding herself, desperate to put some distance between her current life and the guilt over her past. True, it sounded as if, without Veil to stir things up or cater to their worst impulses, his followers appeared to have lost focus and motivation. Yet it was not as if that time was free from instability and

133

suffering. Gary eventually succumbed to his illness and her mum insinuated this might have been the result of some lingering curse placed on him by Veil. She could not forget that Dr Chalk, the local GP, had visited Blackwood Manor on several occasions, although she did not go so far to place him among the worshippers in the woods that night. Then there was the sudden death of the writer Mary Machen. Mother and daughter shared the suspicion that it more than a coincidence she had died whilst visiting Blight to investigate allegations of witchcraft.

What if, throughout this period, Veil's sect had continued to exist in some weakened, damaged state? Maybe there remained, under the skin, old wounds that refused to heal? Some of the older members may have passed away, yet it was always possible younger members had been recruited in their place and were, even now, patiently waiting for the stars to realign in their favour. The letter even included an explicit warning to be cautious around Mrs Stone, who had acted as something like a lieutenant to Veil whilst he was alive. Nevertheless, her mum had attempted to introduce a note of optimism, determined to believe that, in this new era, attitudes had softened and the general threat had abated. Of course, this could again be interpreted as making the best of an impossible situation. Without any funds or family support, it was not as though the Greene family had the option of relocating.

But please don't think I ever put your safety at risk. I did all I could to make the best life for you and your sister. Yet as I watched you grow there were often moments that made me wonder what exactly you had inherited from your father. As much as I hated to admit it at the time there were some aspects of you that reminded me of him. Little things like the faraway look you got in your eye sometimes, as if you were seeing things that nobody else could. Or the way you would disappear for a minute whenever I took my eye off you, especially on an outing or at the bottom of the garden. And what about all those weird objects you collected from the woods to keep on your windowsill? Perhaps you remember the details better than I do but to me they were signs you shared certain things in common with your father. Initially the idea of you inheriting anything from Veil frightened me. Sorry if in reading this the suggestion scares you too. But over time I came to realise, as I hope you will too, that what at first may seem like an affliction or a personality flaw is in fact your greatest strength. Witchcraft is what I am talking about, Tea. Remember how I used to say: 'Bake it, sieve it, knead it, the past is only what you feed it'? Well, that was a little bit of sorcery of my own. What I meant was your gifts are not something that need tie you to the past. Think of them instead as unveiling your future. But if you choose to be a witch, if you accept this as your identity, don't ever feel obliged to adopt 'The Old Ways' with all their negative connotations and tired, narrow minded traditions. This is a great opportunity for you. You could be a new kind of witch! An 'AfterWitch'!

It is not my intention to pressure you into a decision. I know I have already burdened you with far more than you deserve. But, Tea, time may be running out for you to accept your gifts and realise your potential. I hope I am wrong but in the last few years it has sometimes felt as if the old, ugly theories are again taking root in Blight. Complaints are being made about the outside world changing too fast, that things have gone too far. People are saying that it is time to 'take back control'. This is exactly the type of language Veil once used to spread fear throughout the community. And if people are scared, they will soon be seeking scapegoats again. They will be hunting witches like you. Which brings me to my main reason for writing this letter. Tea, if I am no longer around to protect you, you must protect yourself. Be vigilant and be prepared and hope that I am mistaken. For if the tide turns and Veil's coven reasserts itself then all kinds of people will be in danger, but you more than most. Leave the village if you can but be aware there may be barriers. They won't let you go without a fight. Remember, what they lack is a prize that can only be taken from you. The success of their ritual depends upon your blood…

Tea skimmed over the final paragraph, which descended into endless apologies and regrets that, thankfully, she would be able to discuss with her mum later. Then, beneath the signature and kisses, only empty lines. The letter left Tea in complete disarray; exhilarated yet also despondent, shocked yet strangely gratified that everything had turned out to be as suspected. Hadn't people in Blight always looked at her differently? Treated her with reserve and wariness, as if they secretly resented her presence but were reluctant to turn her away? Finally, she knew exactly what 'they', Veil's minions, were after. Certainly not her money or property and, as they must know from local gossip, too late for her virginity. By candle flame, Tea examined her wrists, tracing the blue veins as they snaked down beneath the flesh of her outstretched

135

forearms. Anything else she would have willingly given away. But here was an heirloom she could never dispose of, that she was unable to shed.

Her blood! It was her blood that they wanted!

Chapter Ten: Against the Lore

Tea paced restlessly around the candlelit room, unable to settle, like a moth circling a flame. The blood surged along her veins and into her temples, infusing her with a sense of power yet also threatening to derail her, as though an ungrounded electrical current were pulsing through her body. On almost every circuit she plucked the photograph up from the carpet only to cast it aside again. That man who stood, out of focus, beside her mother, staring from the frame with hollow, uncaring eyes, was the father she had never known! At least Tea now felt she had someone to blame, apart from herself. Yes, it was all his fault! If it were not for Ashton Veil her life could have turned out differently. She would not have felt so rejected and persecuted, that people were forever being dishonest, swimming her like a witch! And now the survivors of his sect were planning to kidnap, to murder her! How, exactly, were you supposed to react in such situations? What were you meant to think? This was all too much for any rational consideration, Tea soon realised. She would need help to hold back this hurricane, to secure her sanity and keep her moored to the real world. She would call Sea; her sister would know what to do.

'Had a bit of a car trouble on the edge of town. Hopefully nothing that can't be fixed! Don't go anywhere, I won't be long. Broke down outside Harrow View House. Will ask for help there. xxx'

Her sister had sent the text a couple of hours ago, presumably whilst Tea was beyond signal in the woods, hence the delay in receipt. Although the wording suggested that Sea was due to arrive any minute, still Tea was reluctant to wait, suspicious as to why there had been no follow up message sent in the intervening period. Yet, as so often happened at 'The Burrows', on dialling back she failed to connect; nothing but a brief spell of dead air, followed by an automated message informing her that Sea's mobile was currently 'unavailable'. Tea swept down the unlit hallway to her own room, brushing aside the trembling shadows and trying her best to ignore the voices in her head.

'What if I am not really who I think I am? What if they substituted babies at the ceremony and my mum stole away a fairy changeling?'

Without stopping to switch on the light, Tea powered up her laptop, bathing the bedroom in an eerie, fluorescent glow. Her intention had been to contact her sister via a different platform, yet a jarring error message immediately lit up the screen, alerting her to a problem with her computer. In her agitated state of mind, it seemed more than a coincidence, an inconvenience, that none of her modes of communication were working. And there was something else. Something that Tea had barely registered when out in the corridor, but which now felt significant. She stepped back to the light switch and flicked it on and off. Nothing; no spark of light as the bulb fused, no dying ember in the filament. Downstairs was also dark; Tea had noticed when she crossed the landing. Yet, earlier, although she had turned out the lights upstairs for that candlelit atmosphere, she was sure she had left them on in the hall and the living room. A power cut? Leaning over the banister, it looked to Tea as if night had descended indoors.

Padding down the stairs, Tea explored silent, ghostly rooms usually so familiar, flicking switches belonging to table lamps and overhead lights without success. Neither the stereo nor television showed any signs of life, yet floorboards creaked in abnormal places. And, all the while, her movements were accompanied by the heart-breaking cries of an invisible cat, Whispers' lament echoing from somewhere impossibly deep below. Tea cursed as she collided with furniture for the umpteenth time. The trouble with 'The Burrows' was that, being so isolated, when it was plunged into darkness it was a proper, primal, pitch-black darkness. There was not even a streetlight for miles. Tea wondered whether it was best to wait for her sister or take a little walk, either part way into the woods or a few minutes along the lane, to see if she could spot any lights in the distance? That would tell her if the problem was restricted to her alone.

Yet, surely Sea would be here soon? The delay could not last much longer? Wishful thinking perhaps, but at that precise moment Tea could have sworn she heard someone approaching the house, the soft tread of footsteps upon the front lawn. She twitched the curtain drawn halfway across the living room window. At first she was greeted solely by her own haunted reflection until, as her eyes adjusted, she was able to see through this pale image painted on glass, into the garden beyond. Furtive activity was taking place out there, robed figures assembling without sound, their presence exposed only when the moon broke from between the clouds. Finally then, the coven had come for her. It was the night of the High Summer Fayre and they were here to lay siege, to claim their sacrificial victim. Stealthily, without need for further exchange, the gathering fanned out to form a half moon around the house. And, one by one, Tea began to pick out faces from the darkness:

Leading the pack, centre stage as always, Mrs Stone strode into view. Her haughty glare and rouged, refined cheekbones remained striking, even when cloaked beneath a heavy hood. A vague gesture or swish of a draped arm was apparently all that was required to conduct proceedings, her subordinates eager to pay heed to her every whim. These silent commands were reinforced by the ever-faithful daughter, Amber, standing proudly at her mother's side. Trailing slavishly in the wake of The Stones, the gloom reducing them to pattering, stooping goblins, Tea recognised Barb Peeks from the library and Robin Dewar, her driving instructor. Meanwhile, obediently taking up their positions on the opposite flank, were Dr Chalk and Nurse Hall, their gaunt, callous expressions still identifiable by moonlight. Amber hissed something in annoyance at Mick Withers from the strawberry farm, sending him scurrying off into the shadows. Ha! So, they were all in it together! Why had she ever doubted herself? To people like Amber, people like Tea would always be expendable, without value. All summer, she had only pretended to be friends. As Tea watched with growing dread, further cult members emerged from the trees, swelling the ranks as they edged towards the sides of the house, aiming to surround the property. Don and Michelle Grade were among them, as was Abigail McRogers and, bringing up the rear, presumably enlisted to provide brawn rather than brains, lumbered Dodsworth from The

Restoration. But to what degree were the pub landlord and Karmilla's embittered landlady involved? What part had been theirs to play?

Before she had time to think this over Tea was distracted by the arrival of two final, unmistakeable figures, completing the congregation. Their advent on the scene appeared to produce a subtle alteration in the atmosphere, perhaps even the hierarchy. Although no more than silhouettes, Tea knew she was looking at the distinct profiles of Elvin and his supposed uncle, the man who went by the name of Mr Tender. Well, if nothing else, at least all that had been kept hidden from her, everything that had been left unsaid, was at last out in the open. Here, on display, was Ashton Veil's true legacy! In spite of the imminent threat, Tea could not help but sneer. These self-appointed leaders of a new, improved world, these guardians of our nostalgia and our heritage, presented such a pitiful, inadequate rabble. Like people say of spiders, they seemed more scared of her than she ought to be of them; witch-hunters waging a hopeless war against anything they did not understand, anything that was not blessed by their first-hand experience. Yet at the same time Tea understood that, just because their resentment was illogical and unfocused, it did not make it any less dangerous. She knew all too well the blind alleys your mind could lead down; the misguided anger, as much as love, that her own disorder could inspire in her. Although, having admitted that, Tea was pretty sure she would never consider wielding her character flaws as a weapon. Would she?

When it came to fight or flight, Tea's first impulse was to flee, yet she knew that by now the coven would have encircled the house, cutting off any avenues of escape. The instant she ventured outside she would fall into their clutches. The only other option was to sit tight; to secure all doors and windows and defend her fortress until her sister arrived. Outside an ominous calm had settled, leading Tea to assume her adversaries were either awaiting her next move or preparing for their decisive onslaught. Aware the clock was ticking, she armed herself with a kitchen knife and, keeping to the shadows, made a quick reconnaissance of the downstairs rooms, barricading any possible, vulnerable access points. Tea accepted her efforts were unlikely to make much of a difference but hoped the deadlocks would hold back the offensive just long enough for Sea to witness what was happening, to call for help. Next, at a loss how best to deploy herself, Tea retreated upstairs once more, surveying the lie of the land from a selection of windows. When she stared unblinking into the night below, she could more or less make out the scattered sentries stationed around the grounds, each paused stock-still, like a standing stone. Tea attempted to tally up their exact number but, every time she tried, she lost count. However, it seemed to her there were now less of them out there than there were before. But, if this were so, then where had the others gone?

A noise from downstairs drew her attention back inside - what sounded like an item of furniture being upturned. Maybe Whispers had found his way home? He had certainly fallen quiet ever since 'The Burrows' had been surrounded. Heart pounding in the hushed gloom, knife raised hesitantly above her head, Tea began to creep back down the stairs, one step at a time. About midway she glanced over the bannister and was barely able to believe what she was seeing. Every inch of the living room was crawling with stifled, squirming activity. Several dark shapes were clumsily yet cautiously forcing themselves up through holes in the floor, dragging their weight across the floorboards. It was as if Tea's house had suddenly given birth to a litter of slithering, subterranean trolls. Despite the efforts of these creatures to remain discreet, everything in sight was disturbed. Rugs and sofas were shoved carelessly to one side, side tables and flower vases were toppled. For a second, Tea's mind struggled to process the evidence presented by her eyes. It was all too absurd. She must have fallen asleep upstairs; this was some Freudian nightmare full of giant slugs and caterpillars. But then, all the elements began to fall into place. The old legends of the tunnels beneath 'The Burrows'; the cries of the cat, echoing as if trapped inside a cave; the barrows of earth that Mr Tender steered back and forth throughout the day. Of course, one of the mysterious tasks the gardener must have set himself was to excavate, to exhume the tunnels that had so long lain forgotten, disused. And now they were re-opened, no household charm could protect her; Veil's followers were worming their way in.

Tea made a bolt for the front door. She was prepared to run all the way to Harrow View House if she had to. Anything to be away from these horrors and safe in the arms of her family. Her mother and sister; her real family. Only it was too late. Before she had a chance to battle with the lock she felt rough hands fall upon her; cold, spindly fingers that gripped like talons, instantly disarming her and hauling her back into the living room. Tea was thrust down into an armchair, which had been displaced from a corner into the middle of the floor. Releasing her from their hold, Tea's captors then swarmed around the chair, looming in close with candles and flashlights as if to interrogate her, offering glimpses of the faces beneath the hoods. In the midst of all the madness, it was nonetheless obvious to Tea that this home invasion had been poorly planned. The half a dozen that had made it inside appeared stunned by their own success, unsure what to do next. Tea watched, bewildered, as the members of this advance party proceeded to bicker over her head, throwing insults and accusations at each other.

"You've made a mistake!" she cut in, close to sobbing in frustration. "I'm not Ashton Veil's daughter! I don't have any special powers! I don't have anything of his!"

"She's lying! That's what women do!" screeched Robin Dewar, only to be cut short by a scathing glance from Mrs Stone.

"I hope you're not going to give us any trouble?" leered Abigail McRogers, her pinched features filling Tea's vision. "Not like that Polish friend of yours, the one who wanted to help you get away. Still, we made sure she wasn't going anywhere, didn't we Dodsworth?"

The pub landlord broke into a broad grin and grunted like a village idiot, chilling Tea to the bone and bringing tears to her eyes. She should have known. Karmilla had never intended to abandon her. Instead she had been abducted, disposed of by this gang of...kidnappers? Lunatics? Murderers?

"If you let me go, I promise I won't say anything..." pleaded Tea. "I'll never come back here. Please just let me leave the village..."

"Leave? You can't leave Blight. Haven't you noticed that yet?" sighed Mrs Stone in exasperation, as though she were addressing a schoolgirl struggling in class. "We've sealed the boundaries to you. Frozen the borderlines. Indeed, that was one of our enchantments that worked a little better. Unlike that unfortunate business with your ex-boyfriend…"

Amber failed to stifle a sob, shrinking back into the shadows to snivel out of sight.

"Evidently, I must have over-egged the love potion in that case…" continued Mrs Stone in a distracted tone, presumably running through the list of ingredients in her head. "We thought he could persuade you to stay but he ended up a liability. The more out of control he became, the more likely it looked he would frighten you off, drive you away before we were ready. That was why he needed to be stopped. A loss to the local community, but I suppose you live and learn. These arts take time to master…"

So, perhaps Jack had not been the enemy, but a victim as much as her? Tea hid her face in her hands, no longer able to place anything in perspective, increasingly sceptical of her own interpretations. As so frequently occurred in times of stress, she was finding it difficult to discern between facts and emotions, to decide which held the truth. All she could be certain of was that she was desperate for space to breathe. She must get out of this room! Out of this house! Away from her hometown, defying whatever restrictions had been placed upon her. Yet her keepers only began to press in closer, tightening the stranglehold of her claustrophobia. From somewhere towards the back, Dr Chalk stepped out of the gloom, brandishing a syringe that he was in the process of filling from a small bottle. Tea was ready to erupt. The malice of those around her had infiltrated her every fibre but, racing to her defence, she felt an intense, uncontrollable energy rising from within.

"Quickly, Chalk, give her something…" urged Mrs Stone. "We must have her under control before we take her to the woods…"

But the doctor got no further before being struck off; felled by a sailing brass coal scuttle that violently impacted with his forehead. The entire living room had abruptly exploded into anarchy. Every single ornament, mirror and unfixed piece of furniture launched itself from its location and became airborne, swirling around in a slipstream, then diving and striking the various cult members repeated blows. Flames leapt to the ceiling from the extinguished fireplace, igniting the fittings. In the chaos, Tea struggled loose from the armchair and darted between the flailing forms of her would-be abductors, all of whom had either been disabled by flying debris or blinded by the thick smoke already filling the room. Her aim had been to reach the back door, yet she too was tricked by the unexpected changes to her home environment. On the verge of escape, suddenly the floor gave way beneath her and Tea found herself tumbling down into one of winding tunnels mined by Mr Tender, dropping from sight like Alice in Wonderland.

In a flash, she hit the bottom, landing in a heap of brushwood and soil. Tea picked herself up and dusted herself down, as relatively unscathed as after the Helter Skelter at the High Summer Fayre. Her enemies must have carried their light sources with them, as down here at night she could barely see a hand raised in front of her face. Yet Tea estimated that the tunnels must not stretch too far, probably leading to the surface at some camouflaged spot in the back garden. Steering herself along the dank walls, often stooped and sometimes crouched on her hands and knees to navigate the narrow passage, she tried not to imagine either what she might be wading through or the nature of the insects that tickled her scalp and scuttled across her splayed fingers. For Tea, the experience recalled fleeting memories of that summer holiday when, first thing every morning, she and her schoolmates had dared each other to crawl into the storm drains beneath the park. Of course all that had come to a halt late August after Dawn Orchard's little brother got hurt and they had to call the fire brigade.

Mercifully, as Tea had anticipated, within five minutes or so a sheen of ailing starlight appeared at the end of the tunnel, guiding her up from the earth and into the garden. A little in advance, Whispers must have escaped the same way. Clambering out into the tropical balm of the evening, Tea was instantly aware of something out of place, a faint illumination infiltrating the expected darkness. Looking back through the foliage, she saw flickering lights in the windows of 'The Burrows', flames catching the curtains of the downstairs rooms. She hesitated; yet there was no time to salvage anything now, no choice but to keep moving. Tea turned with the intention of ploughing forward through the garden, only to be immediately ambushed by the wiry figure of a man, a shape that seemed to spring forth from the shadows. She felt herself gripped in a rigid embrace from which she was unable to break free, the few feeble kicks and punches she threw quickly restrained.

"And where do you think you're going, Miss Felicity?"

Dreaming of escape, she had almost forgotten about Mr Tender. The gardener crowed softly to himself as he lifted Tea off her feet and began to convey her back towards the burning house, apparently revelling in her perceived submission. Nevertheless, despite her seemingly helpless situation, Tea sensed a gentle shift in the balance of power, as though, in secret, she was now the one left holding the cards. Yes, Mr Tender may think he held the advantage over her but, lately, Tea had learnt all kinds of things that he remained ignorant of. For one, she was in on his act and had proof he was not the man he claimed to be. Secondly, she now knew, for certain, that she had the ability to summon up psychic forces of her own. The conflagration in the living room. There could be no mistake; she had caused that.

'There is no point in fighting 'The Old Ways', Felicity…'" sermonised Mr Tender as he strolled down the path, his voice serene and beginning to shed its fake, rustic twang. "That's just the way things are. The way things should always be…"

Clasped so close to his chest, cheek pressed against cheek, Tea at last felt as if Mr Tender's mask was slipping, that she could see through his disguise. And, underneath it all, lay something elusive yet vaguely familiar. A hint of a face she knew or had once known. Perhaps a figure from her distant past or simply someone she passed in the street every day without giving them a second thought? Tea searched her mind for the duplicate image, the lost twin. Where had she seen that same mirthless glint of the eye, the same arrogant turn of the lip? Maybe…no, it couldn't be? Maybe…the man in the photograph with her mother?

Tea was shaken by the idea, even as a mere possibility; fleetingly fascinated yet instinctively repelled. Locked in the arms of this unknown man she felt the now familiar storm brewing up inside herself, the tell-tale signs that once she would have mistaken for signs of her personality disorder. A tide of intense emotions coursed through her, wild and overwhelming and yet, for the first time, perhaps no longer beyond her control. Tea focused intently upon the torrent, channelling her thoughts into a modulated tremor that reverberated through her entire frame and seemed to spill out into the world around her, resonating through the trees. The gardener was taken by surprise, ejected by an invisible force that sent him sprawling into the flower beds, stunned into semi-consciousness. Tea too hit the ground, but was back on her feet within seconds, knowing this would be her only chance of freedom. Mr Tender also tried to rise, but an apparently twisted ankle pulled him back down into the undergrowth, folding him over with a cry of pain. Tea took to her heels without looking back, careering recklessly through nettle patches and roses bushes, blinded by the night.

"You won't get far Felicity!" The gardener's voice roared, defiantly, in her wake. "You'll find the garden isn't quite as you remember…"

His words had the desired effect on Tea, instantaneously conjuring up images from the afternoon of Elvin's attack, when she had got lost outside in what felt like an alternate universe. She recalled how she had failed to recognise her own back garden; the unknown plants that seemed to have taken root overnight, the air of menace that had settled over the grounds like a heat haze. And tonight, it was happening again.

146

Previously, Tea would have been able to gauge the twists and turns with her eyes closed; she had even managed it after sinking two bottles of wine. Yet now her trusty inner compass had gone askew. Every choice she made brought her up against an impassable wall of greenery, every path she took either tapered out or led back towards 'The Burrows'. The disorientation was even worse in the darkness; Tea found it impossible to sustain her sense of direction. And, all the while, she was sure her pursuers must be gaining ground, almost upon her. Were those glow-worms concealed deep within the briar? Or the glint of Elvin's green eyes as he silently crawled towards her through the scrub?

In her agitation, Tea began to imagine all sorts of wayward things. Retaliating against her attempts to hack and hew her way through the vegetation, the tendrils of monstrous flowers appeared to coil around her ankles, trying to trip her up and drag her down. Vines and creepers wound themselves around her waist, her thighs, and refused to let go. 'They won't let me leave!' she panicked. 'They want to keep me here! They want to preserve my bloodline!' If this was no dream, if this was really happening, Tea knew it must be another enchantment performed by Mr Tender. Aside from digging tunnels beneath her house, he had also occupied his time hexing her garden, transforming it into uncharted, enemy territory. She needed to think fast, or risk being marooned in Blight forever, if not a fate even worse. Tea screwed her eyes shut and searched inside herself for an answer...

'Well, that was a little bit of sorcery of my own...'

An extract from her mum's letter suddenly popped into Tea's head. What exactly had been that 'little bit of sorcery' again? Wait. Wasn't it that ridiculous phrase her mum always used to repeat? The same one that Tea had happened to utter in The Veil House, before she unearthed the key from the roots? Maybe her mum had more of a gift, more of a knowledge of magic than she was letting on? Could this actually be the opening line of an authentic spell? Tea, with nothing to lose, decided it was worth a try.

147

"Bake it, sieve it, knead it. The past is only what you feed it…" she shakily declared out loud.

The result was dramatic yet almost imperceptible to the naked eye; as if the dark had been gently parted like the heavy folds of a stage curtain, a tiny rift appearing in the velvet fabric of the night. All at once, Tea saw her way forward. She tore her way through an obstinate, seemingly endless citadel of hostile foliage, cages of gnarled branches and serrated hedgerows, before eventually arriving, bruised and bloodied, on the little trail that cut across the foot of the garden. From here she could reach the woods…

Finally, those hunting her were left far behind. Yet, for a while, Tea could still hear them, even as she increased her distance. Their laments carried on the light summer breeze, faint voices sounding evermore desperate and confused:

"Where has she gone? I don't understand! Where has she gone?"

"I'm sorry, why are you asking me? Am I supposed to know everything???"

"But…the spell? How did she get away?"

"That is no longer my responsibility!"

****

A nocturnal mirage of HarmWood shimmered before Tea's eyes: a double exposure of dense thickets and deep-set groves. Everything appeared unfixed, a drift in the landscape. Perhaps she should have paid greater attention to her path, yet all the time she was running her mind had also been racing, swamped by the innumerable implications and potential outcomes of the discoveries she had made. And now she was no longer sure where she was or where she was going, out of breath in the middle of nowhere. If only she could call Sea or her mum to talk things over, to be reassured that the cover stories and half-truths of the past could now be laid to rest. Yet Tea was without a phone, having dropped it during the struggle at 'The Burrows', meaning that most likely it had gone up in flames, along with all her other possessions. Talk about burning your bridges! She felt like some abandoned, orphaned creature cast out into the night, a satellite adrift in a strange orbit.

Come to think of it, Tea realised that, for some time now, she had been aware of subtle changes taking place in her surroundings. Since when, exactly? Well, on reflection…ever since she had resorted to witchcraft to escape the back garden. If only she been given a chance to consider the consequences, maybe even the opportunity for a little covert research in the Restricted Reading Room. But the danger had been pressing and probably still was; it would not take long to track her route through the woods. Whilst accepting it was too late for regrets, Tea was nevertheless unsettled by the thought of what she might have unleashed. From the point she had invoked her powers it had felt as if the world around her was slowly but steadily filling up with wild magic, like she had walked away from a running tap. The simplest things were suddenly imbued with a new meaning, a hidden depth, causing Tea to question her senses. Empty spaces felt full of frenetic activity, like a hive; perspectives and boundaries were becoming blurred. Had her spell broken her ties with Blight or merely freed her from the confines of the garden? If she reached the edge, would she still find an invisible barrier holding firm, preventing her from leaving the village? Considering they had kept Tea under such strict surveillance and had concocted such an intricate plot to ensure her captivity, from her mum's mysterious illness to a failed driving test and near financial ruin, it seemed unlikely that Veil's allies would simply allow their web to unravel. Surely they would not let their prey slip away unchallenged? Yet there was more to this magic than perhaps they had accounted for. It was not only externally Tea had begun to discern a shift, but internally too. What shape would this transformation take? In her current mood anything seemed possible. She had been cut loose and everything was up in the air, a host of incarnations available.

Tea whispered her secret into a gaping hole in a tree trunk, grinning slyly to herself. But what does an AfterWitch do? Where does she go?

Her ruminations were interrupted by a slight disturbance in the bracken up ahead. Tea froze on the spot, before releasing a gasp of joy. What she had seen was a squat figure bounding freely back and forth between pools of dark until, aware of her presence, it had halted, bristled and pricked up its ears. Hopscotch! As with Noosha on the other side of the woods, the hare had clearly responded to Tea's silent distress call, volunteering to lead her out of the darkness. Not a moment too soon, thought Tea, for she could hear the enemy forces advancing behind her, flattening the woodland with their heavy tread. 'Follow me', Hopscotch seemed to suggest as she flipped around and fled deep into HarmWood, the image of which once again appeared to tremble like the surface of a lake, a ripple effect that warned Tea not to trust her eyes. Yet the remnants of Ashton Veil's company were closing in and she had no choice but to open her mind, to accept whatever ploy Hopscotch was proposing. Tea chased after the hare, mimicking every feint and zigzag it made, just as she had done with Noosha. But this time something felt different, something strange was happening…

Whereas as before Tea had struggled to keep pace with the fox, on this occasion she found herself effortlessly picking up speed, taking flight through nocturnal scenery. A rolling vista of silhouetted trees flashed past, like images cast by a magic lantern. It was as though she were riding the breeze on a broomstick, swooping briskly over unsteady terrain and dipping elegantly to avoid any obstacle in her path. And yet, at other moments, Tea felt as if she were leaping and skipping alongside Hopscotch, sprinting neck and neck through the woodland, their shadows merging so close to the ground. The two had become interchangeable, intertwined. Suddenly, she was no longer alongside the animal but inside, sharing a soul, sharing a skin. Tea could barely contain a cry of glee. Just like in days of old, she was a witch who could turn into a hare! Hopscotch was her familiar, her spirit guide, her other half. A missing link that had been restored! Tea somersaulted head over heels, chasing the moon as it sailed above in swift momentum, accompanied by dark clouds scudding towards an unknown end. If, at intervals, cloaked figures would try and waylay her, would attempt to interrupt her pleasure, she always proved too quick for them. Tea slipped from their grasp when they burst from the trees and evaded the savage traps set in the undergrowth. Yes, she left them all for dead, muttering bitterly under their breaths as they staggered around their plots in ever decreasing circles.

So, this is what it means to be an AfterWitch! Now that Tea was outside she felt liberated, free of all the petty cruelties and narrow prejudices that had been forced upon her. In this new realm she could originate a witchcraft of her own, independent of her father's shadow and ignoring his rules, operating against the lore. And this alchemy, this blood, she would share with anyone who expressed an interest, until the day came when there would be no more magicians in the world, only magic. Eyes fixed fiercely ahead, Tea swerved into the left-hand path, knowing this was the route she was destined to take…

Up through the trees she spied a pale strip of paved lane, looking out of place but sparkling celestially beneath the stars. And waiting there in stern, expectant silence, stood a black hansom cab, polished and complete with ebony horses and muffled, unheeding groom. Tea emerged from the woods to discover she had resumed her human form. On cautiously approaching the carriage, she had the feeling that everything about this encounter had been preordained. With the soft click of a latch the door swung open. Inside, two passengers reclined in the shadows, dressed in what appeared to be gowns of old-fashioned silk. Was that really her sister, beckoning Tea to join them inside with a wave like royalty? And could that be her mother, nestled in the gloom behind Sea, a wan smile playing on her lips as she gently stroked a cat resembling Whispers, curled up in her lap? This is like a scene from a fairy-tale, marvelled Tea. They must have leased the carriage and the clothes from Harrow View House after the car broke down; that seemed to be the appropriate coat of arms emblazoned on the side.

But why look any closer? At least, tonight, she would finally be leaving Blight in style. Tea placed one foot up on the carriage step, content, for now, to be lost in a daze. Later, during the journey, she could plan for her future and, almost as importantly, redress the past.

'Whatever I was before, underneath I was always an AfterWitch...'

AfterWitch
'A Sense of Foreboding on a Summer's Evening'
By James Stoorie
March-October 2020

About the Author:

James Stoorie was born in 1972.
He is still not dead.

https://jamesstoorie.wordpress.com/

https://twitter.com/JamesStoorie

https://www.instagram.com/jamesstoorie

https://www.facebook.com/james.stoorie.31

Printed in Great Britain
by Amazon

82524573R00092